Return of White Buffalo

Book I

A Series
Created and Written
By
Charles Fivekiller Breul

CHARLES FIVEKILLER BREUL

Camelot Publishing
P.O. Box 500057
Lake Los Angeles, Ca.93535
E-Mail camelotpublishing@hotmail.com

First Edition 2006

Library of Congress Control Number 2005931344

ISBN # 0-9754063-5-3

Cover art "His Devine Presence" Through the courtesy of Lee
Cable. www.leecableart.com

Editor: Lorri Schafnitz

Native American Icons through the courtesy of Poison's Icons

Reviews

By our Native American Peers
In their own words

Not long ago, I was handed a book titled *The Return of White Buffalo* and asked to read it and give my opinion of its content.

In my opinion, "This book should be read by everyone." I found it inspiring and written from the heart, no book I have ever read has inspired me such as this.

Although a book of fiction, its contents are much true, as it deals with what we Native Americans deal with in our everyday lives, spirituality, love, friendship, sharing and family relationships, which more of us need to understand, instead of fighting amongst ourselves. I feel this book is a must for all our people, to open their eyes and their hearts, to help them examine their selves and I hope this book touches them as it touched me. I feel Charles was inspired by the Great Spirit to send this message to us all, not only Native Americans, but to the world. I hope it inspires you as much as it inspired me.

Alesander Littlebow
Mescalero Apache

Stoney is simply astounding! He portrays all that is right and fundamentally true in regards to the old ways of those of us who are, referred to as Native Americans. A true warrior: courageous, keen of mind, and compassionate of heart. These are just a few of the praises that flood through my mind for *White Buffalo*.

Wesley Edminister
Jamestown S'Klallam Band
of the Klallam Nation

When I began reading *Return of White Buffalo,* I did not know it would bring out a spirit within me I didn't know even existed.

The description of the people and places were so vivid, I felt I was actually there. I stayed up until almost midnight reading this book, because I felt a great anticipation and did not want to put it down. Even knowing this book was fiction it instilled a deep feeling of truth in the history and culture of the Native American people and their beliefs. It inspired me to examine my own heritage; it made me proud to be a Native American, and left me wanting more.

Mary A. Weber
Cherokee (And proud of it)

I'm not much of a reader, unless it's about powwows, hunting, fishing or beading. So when I first met Charles at one of our powwows and he handed me a book and asked me to let him know what I thought of it. I was not really sure I wanted to do this, but I said I would and I'm glad I did. As I believe, most all Native Americans should read this book. It will come close to their hearts. Things in this book could be them in real life as they are in mine. The spirituality brought out in this book is something all Native Americans need to understand and believe, or it will be lost as so many other of our beliefs are being lost. All people, of all color, need to understand our Indian beliefs.

Let all people keep the Great Spirit in their hearts every day of their lives, not just on Sundays.

When people walk into the ring of life and dance, it inspires their body and renews their belief in our Creator.

This book is easy to read and easy to understand.

Thank you Charles
Billy Yarbrough
Choctaw

An Open Letter to our People

Several of my Native American friends have been wondering why I would take it upon myself to write such novels as the *White Buffalo* series. One such friend has taken offense at my using the White Buffalo, one of the most sacred symbols of our Native American legends, as the mainstay of the *White Buffalo* novels.

I would like to take this opportunity to explain why I felt I had to write the *White Buffalo* series and why I felt it was important for me to use the sacred White Buffalo, which I would never intentionally dishonor.

I know many will say, "He did it for the money," and, while to an extent this may be true, it is only partially so, for the decision to write this book did not come easily. I thought long and hard and searched my conscious extensively before I set one word to paper.

I thought about all the books about native people I have read throughout my life, depicting them as savages, drunks, or dumb, lazy, second rate citizens. And how, even today, when many people hear the words Native American, they still have images of an Indian picking up discarded empty beer cans along a busy highway or primitive people living in Hogan's, Wicki-ups, and Tepees.

I thought about how our youngsters go to school and read biased history books telling distorted stories of how our people were defeated in their quest to protect their families, homes, and their way of life or they go to the movies and actually cheer as a troop of cavalry led by John Wayne slaughters, hundreds of our people. When I see this happening, I ask myself, where have all our warriors gone?

Our children have been and are being brain washed to such an extent that many of them are actually denying their heritage. This is wrong and it pains me deeply, for their heritage, should not be abandoned - it should be celebrated.

Our children should be standing tall and be proud to say, "I'm Native American."

Our youngsters are our future; they are our warriors of tomorrow and we must arm them with knowledge, not the antiquated arms of yesteryear, for the battles they will face will require knowledge, not arms. As Chief Leonard Crowdog, whom I am honored to say fully supports the "*Return of White Buffalo*", recently said to me, "Our children walking this earth today are what should be most important to us all."

Our warrior ancestors fought for centuries to protect their families and their way of life. They thought nothing of giving their lives for what they believed in, and never believed we could be defeated by anyone.

We, the original people have always been like *heartwood* - the older we get, the stronger our core becomes.

This is why I felt it was important for me to write the *White Buffalo* series. I felt I should explain to our youngsters that what they read in their history books, see in the movie theaters, and watch on their television sets is not necessarily the way it happened. I wanted to explain to our youngsters that we were never the savages the biased media has portrayed us.

We did not believe in butchering or killing anyone. We believed, if we took a life, it became our responsibility to care for and look after the deceased's family. This is why our warrior ancestors, used the coup stick, a long, decorated, and hooked stick, much like a Shepherd's staff. For nothing exhibited, a warrior's bravery more than to ride into battle armed with nothing more than his coup stick, for nothing shamed an enemy more than to have an enemy warrior strike him with his coup stick. Many true warriors would have preferred death rather than be laughed at while stories were told around campfires of his being vanquished by a warrior armed with only a coup stick.

This is the way our warriors fought our battles before the invading hordes of European immigrants began taking our land, enslaving, and slaughtering our people.
We suddenly found our coup sticks were no longer effective against these armed, land hungry barbarians from another land, who thought nothing of killing and raping our women and yes even our children.

My great-great-great grandmother proudly fought alongside her warrior husband in several battles to protect their home and family from these invaders, and while others may call her savage, I think of her as loving and brave, and feel, honored to have such ancestors, who would fight to their death to protect what, was theirs.

I wanted to create a modern day Native American warrior our youngsters could feel akin to, a modern day warrior who lived by the four tenets our ancestor warriors have always lived by fortitude, generosity, bravery, and wisdom.

A modern day warrior who was unafraid to express spirituality, who was unafraid to show a deep love of his family and his fellow human beings, a modern day Native American warrior who was confident in himself and unafraid to show compassion to others.

A modern day Native American warrior, who refuses to forget his great heritage, a modern day Native American warrior our youngsters could both look up to and emulate,.

A modern day warrior our youngsters could be proud of, and yes, they have much to be proud of, for they are the original people, the first Americans.

As our youngster's elders, it is our responsibility to never allow them to forget how wonderful their heritage is, for if we fail our youngsters, we fail our ancestors.

I welcomed this opportunity to shed the light of truth on a few of the many atrocities, Native Americans have had inflicted on them throughout the years - atrocities such as Wounded Knee, The Trail of Tears, Washita, Sand Creek, The Long Walk, the Marias Massacre, and the Massacre of Tohopeka.

Atrocities our youngsters have probably never heard of, yet bring tears to my eyes whenever I think of the suffering that atrocities such as these have caused our people. Yes, I welcomed the opportunity to tell these stories, not as our distorted history books tell them, but to be able to tell of them as they actually happened, as told by their survivors not biased journalists or disillusioned screen writers.

I also intend telling the truth about America's death camps, death camps worse than Auschwitz or Dachau ever were. Where over a period of almost a hundred years, tens and tens of thousands of our children were enslaved, beaten, raped, sodomized and murdered. Children as young as four and five years old raped and sodomized on a regular basis under the guise of Christianizing and educating our children.

A true story so horrible I don't look forward to telling it, but I will tell it, for I believe it's time this story of how our children were being brainwashed for almost a hundred years, with our Government's blessing, must be told, for our youngster's deserve the truth.

Yes, I felt it was important to write the *White Buffalo* series, and I felt I needed the power of the White Buffalo to reach our youngsters. Many of whom have never realized how wonderful their heritage actually is or how proud they should be of being Native Americans and if the *White Buffalo* can awaken this pride in even one of our youngsters, I believe the Great Spirit would approve.

Respectfully
Charles Fivekiller Breul
Author *"Return of White Buffalo" Book I*

P.S.   As it is my intention to weave one or two of these atrocities into each White Buffalo episode, I would appreciate hearing any suggestions you may have, regarding true stories, you believe should be included in the *White Buffalo* series.

E-mail your suggestions to camelotpublishing@hotmail.com along with, any information you may have, or reference to establishing its authenticity, and together we will tell our youngsters the truth.

In Honor of Jenny Fivekiller a
Beloved Woman with a Warriors Heart

Table of Contents

		Traditional People	13
Chapter	1	The Rainbolt	17
Chapter	2	Black Eagle Valley	23
Chapter	3	Granite Peaks	31
Chapter	4	The Vision	37
Chapter	5	The Hunters	47
Chapter	6	Storm over Granite Peaks	53
Chapter	7	Hunters Return	61
Chapter	8	The Quest	69
Chapter	9	Lou's Café	73
Chapter	10	Wishing on a Star	81
Chapter	11	Timmy Morris	91
Chapter	12	The Truck Stop	97
Chapter	13	Little Cotton Picker	109
Chapter	14	The Carnival	121

Table of Contents continued

Chapter 15   The Rodeo   129

Chapter 16   Hayes Carlin   137

Chapter 17   The Bulls   149

Chapter 18   The Skinwalker Vision   157

Chapter 19   Evening Star   173

Chapter 20   Talking Drums   181

Chapter 21   Gathering of Nations   185

Chapter 22   Mountain Chant Healing Ceremony   195

Chapter 23   Return of White Buffalo   201

Sitting Bull would ask, where have all our warriors gone?

Traditional People

For over a hundred and sixty years, so called intellectuals, including Darwin, in report after report, claimed no religion existed among Native American Indians.

Considering spirituality plays such a major part in the everyday life of every Native American, this author finds such a statement from otherwise intelligent men bordering on the ridiculous.

I believe such a fallacy can only, be attributed to the fact that no word existed in Indian tongue for the word "religion." Along with the intellectual's lack of fully understanding, the Indian people and their beliefs, coupled with the blinding of their own religious beliefs. Simply because we did not believe as they believed.

While in fact, our belief in a Supreme Being predates even the Christian belief in the Christ child. As with the Christian, Jewish and Muslim religions, our beliefs, were passed down to us since the beginning of time. Through the guardians of our past, our holy men and elders, as were our ceremonies, legends and folklore

Spirituality is as much a part of every Traditional Native American as breathing. However because we may balk at entering under a black robes, expensive roof, to worship, at his man made, shiny gold gilded altars cluttered with his man made golden chalices, they call us heathens. In much the same tone as the baby stealers used when they called us, "Godless savages," as they tore our babies from their mother's breast to give to one of their many wives to bring up in their so-called Christian ways.

Yes, they call us heathens to this very day, because we want to worship in our own way, the way our ancestors have worshipped for thousands of years.

To be able to experience a sunrise over our Creators magnificent desert on a bright spring morning, watching his beautiful desert explode with wild flowers of every imaginable color.

To be able to stroll through a meadow in the early morning hours, and see the tiny dewdrops glistening on his emerald green spring grasses, sparkling in the sunlight as if they were a billion brilliant diamonds.

To be able to wander through his forests or sit beside one of his sparkling brooks and watch his beautiful wild creatures scamper about.

To be able to climb one of his mighty mountains to watch one of his spectacular sunsets, one so beautiful you know in your heart that no one could have possibly created it, except our Creator.

These are his altars, his cathedrals, where we feel most comfortable worshiping, where we feel closest to him.

Where, we feel as if we were one with his earth, one with his creatures, and one with our beloved Creator.

If you doubt these words, I only ask you visit one of his cathedrals next Sunday morning, spend a few minutes gazing at the magnificent beauty he has created for us. Think about him, and allow yourself the pleasure of feeling his presence, for he is there as he is there, for us all. Listen to him, listen to his voice in the wind as it gently flows through the trees, talk to him, talk to him with your heart.

Now I ask who among us is to say our beliefs are wrong. Or in our own way, we are not all worshiping the same Supreme Being, the same Great Spirit, the same Creator, and the same Wakan Tonka?

As traditional people, all we ask is that we be allowed to worship in our own way, the way our ancestors worshiped.

Not as your black robes say we must worship, for they tell us we must worship as they worship, if we expect to go to heaven. What they fail to understand is we do not want to go to their heaven; we want to go to the other side, for that is where our ancestors await us, in the spirit world. And yes, I truly believe there is a Spirit World and know in my heart that is where our loved ones await us.

The way of traditional people is open to all, if you can open your heart and truly believe as we believe, speak to your elders, spiritual advisers and holy men, be proud of being Native Americans and know in your heart, we are truly the first Americans, we are the original people.

While Stony Wood may very well be a character of fiction, I will not say the legend of the White Buffalo is fiction, as the White Buffalo is part of our heritage and as Black Eagle tells us in our story. The *Adawehsi* (Dreamers) were telling stories of the White Buffalo before the Great Buzzard flew across our country, making the Great Smokies, before the Great Buzzard even learned to fly.

Now I ask why this should be harder to believe than the parting of the seas, the burning bush, or the golden tablets found by Joseph Smith.

While I created Stony Wood as a character of fiction, the characters of John Wood and Peggy Wood are only partially fictional. As John Wood is both, named and styled after my own grandfather, and Peggy Wood in memory of my own dear mother. Many of the names of fictional characters in this book are actually names of many of my dear friends. It is my hope, when they read their names in any of my books they will know they are also in my heart.

The names I use for horses throughout the White Buffalo series are names of horses I have had the pleasure to personally possess and love throughout my life.
The Author...

Dedication

Such a book as this from the White Buffalo series can only be dedicated to one group of people, those who have made this series of books possible in my heart.

I therefore dedicate this book to the tens and tens of thousands of Native Americans of every tribe across this great land of ours, the Americas, from the tip of Panama to the frozen tundra of Alaska. To all people, who have never lost heart, and who will always be proud and stand a little taller, whenever they have the opportunity to say, "I'm Native American."

1

The Rainbolt

On what has become an almost typical Saturday afternoon in Norman, Oklahoma, while a crisp breeze is snapping hundreds of brightly colored pennants and flags above the Oklahoma Memorial Stadium a standing room only crowd of over 82,000 football fans are stomping their feet and shouting their lungs out, cheering their teams to victory.

The excitement and enthusiasm of this critical game, deciding the important Big Twelve championship between the Oklahoma Sooners and the Texas Longhorns, can be felt in the electrically charged atmosphere throughout the stadium. The Longhorns lead the Sooners by a score of 20 to 17, with less than a minute to play. The Sooners have the ball on their 30 yard line and now have just called a time out. But no one has gone to the sideline to confer with their coaches.

With the two school bands trying to out play each other and the cheerleaders on both sidelines cheering their heads off, one shouting "Defense, Defense" while the other is shouting "Go. Go". The stadium seems to tremble with excitement as the entire student body from both schools are on their feet, shouting encouragement, waving their pennants, jumping up and down, and stomping their feet.

The play-by-play announcer, shouting into his microphone, can barely be heard over what can only be described as total pandemonium. "I don't understand it; in all my years of broadcasting, I've never seen anything like this...

Wood called a time out, but no one came to the sideline. The coaches sent in a substitute, but he was waved off before he even stepped on the field.

The coaches are standing on the sideline, shaking their heads with their hands on their hips as if they were trying to figure out what's going on, while the Sooners gather around in a big loose huddle.

But it's not really a huddle... It's more like a big pep rally...And—That's exactly what it is, a big mid-field pep rally. We've just turned a directional mic on their huddle. Their patting each other on the back, cheering each other on and, if you can believe this, they're actually growling at each other and four of them are – are doing, what looks like a war dance. And listen to the fans, they love it, they're going wild. Now the Oklahoma fans are starting their own war dance, they're dancing up and down the aisles.

I can't believe what I'm seeing... The Sooners have been playing football here since 1895 and I don't believe there has ever been a game to compare with this...

There's the whistle ending the time out and the Sooners form a huddle... a real huddle. It's third and eight with less than a minute to go and the Sooners come out of the huddle with a roar, or should I say growl. They go into an unbalanced line and there's the snap... Wood is dropping back to the twenty, -- the fifteen... He's looking for a receiver... The crowds in the stands are suddenly silent. You could almost hear a pin drop... Whew... I thought they had him... He turns up field... He's going to run it and look at that block and there's another. His blockers are clearing the way... He's at the forty, the fifty." And suddenly pandemonium breaks out in the stands. The stadium trembles with excitement as everyone begins jumping up and down, cheering and screaming.. .

"Another great block and he's at the forty. And.. and they broke him loose"…Shouting… "He's going all the way... Touchdown!"

The stadium goes wild, fans stamping their feet, waving their pennants and cheering as loud as they possibly can.

Meanwhile, in the great room of the almost six hundred and fifty thousand acre Rainbolt Ranch, John Wood, an American Indian in his late forties, with black wavy hair with a little silver along his temples is having a few business associates and their wives over to watch the Sooners and his son Stoney on the 50" wide screen T.V..

John is out of his chair, jumping up and down like a young kid, cheering his son on. "Go… Go, Goooo… Did you see that? Did you see that? Did you ever see anything like that in your entire life?" Pausing as if daring anyone to disagree, "I can't believe that run. What a game…"

Williams, Fifties, white hair, southern and stuffy. "Yes, I can definitely see why you're so proud of that boy."

Phil, mid forties, pear shaped and bald. "I have to tell you John, I really didn't think Oklahoma could beat Texas, but they pulled it off in real style."

David, fifties, tall and gray hair, sipping on a margarita, asks, "Didn't Stoney make All American?"

With a proud look John answers. "Two years in a row."

Phil nods his head. "Good for him. I hope I get a chance to meet him in person."

Grinning, like proud fathers do, "Well you're all coming out to the ranch to go hunting next Saturday and Stoney doesn't have a game next week, I'll ask him if he'd like to join us."

Twirling the crushed ice in his almost empty margarita glass, Phil nods his head. "That sounds great John, I'll be looking forward to meeting him."

John's wife Peggy, a tall, slim regal looking, very attractive Native American woman in her early forties, with high cheekbones and long raven black hair almost to her waist, walks over to the men and asks, "Would you gentlemen like something to eat, or maybe something to drink?"

John turns and with a smile for his wife says, "Have one of the maids do that honey."

"Nonsense John, I enjoy doing it,"

Peggy picks up some dishes and empty glasses, turns and leaves the room.

Watching her leave, John smiles as he says affectionately,. "She thinks it's silly to have maids when she's perfectly able to do things herself. She even insists on doing most of the cooking around here and I must admit it's tastier than what that high priced cook of ours makes."

Later that evening Peggy is setting John's dinner on the kitchen table when Stoney, tall, handsome, muscular with coal black hair almost to his broad shoulders, walks in wearing an old faded pair of wranglers, scuffed cowboy boots, a well worn western shirt, and a beat up western hat. He's carrying a blue canvas athletic bag.

"Am I in time for dinner?"

Smiling at her son, "As always, your timing is perfect. Have a seat."

Setting the blue bag on the floor by the table, Stoney turns to his mother, puts his arms around her and kisses her on her forehead. With a slight blush Peggy smiles and gently pushes her son away. "Now go on and sit down before your dinner gets cold."

Laughing, Stoney takes a seat next to his father who, with obvious pride in his son, places his hand on his son's hand.

I couldn't believe that game. I got so excited I was jumping up and down like a little kid. You were great Stoney and I'm proud of you."

"Wait a minute Dad, I didn't do it all by myself. I had a lot of help out there. If the guys hadn't blocked for me the way they did, Texas would have smeared me."

Laughing, "I knew you were going to say something like that and of course, you're right. But it was still a great game and I'm still proud of you.

Peggy puts his dinner on the table and takes a seat across from her two men. Stoney reaches down, picking up the blue bag, and handing it to his father.

Opening the bag, "What's this?" John asks as he opens the bag.

"It's the game ball, and when I told the guys I was going to give it to you; they all wanted to sign it. So I guess you can say it's from all of us."

Looking at the ball in silence, with happiness glistening in his eyes, John says, "Thanks Stoney and thank the guys for me." Tossing the ball in the air, "I think I'm going to have a special trophy case made for this."

With a twinkle in her eye, while still trying to sound stern, Peggy say's. "Now I want both of you to put your toys away and eat your dinner before it gets cold."

Laughing, Stoney say's, "All right mom, I am in a little hurry this evening. I promised Grandpa Rainbolt I'd come by early this evening."

"That's good, I baked a chicken and some homemade biscuits for him, so you can take a basket to him, and be sure he eats it while it's hot."

John's shaking his head. "I don't know why he insists on living out there by himself. He's almost seventy years old and he should be here with us, so we can take care of him."

Glancing at his father, "He doesn't want to be taken care of, he wants to take care of himself and live in the old ways..."

"Stoney's right, he wouldn't have even let you build a house for him if I hadn't put my foot down." Peggy says in agreement.

Shaking his head, John say's, "A house, it's not really a house, it's a log cabin."

"It's a long house, built in the tradition of the old ways. He's happy there and he has his tepee, sweat lodge, and a ceremonial arena." Stoney explains.

Yes, and "And I hear he's still having ceremonial dances." John exclaims.

"Of course he is. He's a Holy Man and that's part of his heritage… It's part of our heritage!" Stoney says, in defense of his grandfather.

"I know he's been instructing you since before you were even five yeas old, but after all the education you've had, do you really believe in all that spirit stuff?"

"Of course I believe, I've seen the spirits and I can feel their presence with me in everything I do."

Shaking his head…"I thought you'd grow out of that as you got older, especially with your education."

"Education doesn't have anything to do with it and it's not anything I'll ever grow out of, because it's part of my heritage too. A heritage I'm proud of and I often wish you could feel what I feel."

Listening to an argument she's heard a thousand times, Peggy shakes her head.. "Now that's enough from both of you about our heritage. I don't like to hear you two arguing about something that's so important to all of us."

Getting up from the table, "I'll get the chicken and biscuits, ready for your grandfather and you better tell him I want him to eat it while it's hot and I'll put a little honey in for the biscuits."

While his mother is fixing a basket for him to take to his grandfather, his father gets up from the table tossing the football in the air, "I'll just set this on the mantle for now."

2

Black Eagle Valley

The narrow dirt road wanders around and up a little hill, where it suddenly ends. Stoney pulls his 4-wheel drive pickup to the side of the road where he parks and, getting out, picks up the basket his mother sent to her father. Then walks to the edge of the cliff where he can look down on Black Eagle's camp, Black Eagle Valley

It so peaceful, it is almost mystical, with its artesian well coming out of the side of the mountain creating a little waterfall, cascading into a pool at the foot of the mountain, a little stream shaded by huge cottonwood, trees wandering down the valley. Just beyond the stream, a ceremonial dance arena and a sweat lodge set to one side near the pool. Black Eagle's tepee is on a little knoll above the dance arena and a little log, long house is about a hundred yards beyond the tepee. A few horses and cattle can be seen lazily grazing on the lush green grass in the meadow beyond the cabin.

As Stoney starts down the winding narrow path, he notices a fire burning in the center of the dance arena, and several people moving around outside the sacred circle. When he reaches the little stream, he barely manages to get across without getting his boots wet, by leaping from stone to stone to stone. Walking around the arena, he notices his grandfather sitting in front of the tepee, holding his sacred pipe.

Black Eagle is a tall man in his late sixties with long snow-white hair wrapped in ermine skins. Wearing a soft deerskin shirt, decorated with brightly, colored beads and matching breeches, moccasins, a bone choker and a bright red turban. Watching his grandson approach, Black Eagle rises, motioning for Stoney to follow him into the tepee.

The floor of the tepee is covered with animal skins, while brightly colored feathers, beads, dream catchers, gourds and tortoise shell rattles hang from the lodge poles. Small bundles of sage and sweet grass, drying on the walls, fill the lodge with its sweet aroma. A small fire is burning in the center of the floor, its little whiff of smoke slowly drifting up and out the smoke hole.

Stoney steps into the tepee and stops to remove his boots and slip into a pair of moccasins Black Eagle sits by the fire and motions Stoney to sit across from him. Setting the basket down, he sits across from his grandfather, nodding toward the basket.

"Morning Dove sent dinner for you, and told me` I was to be sure you ate it while it was still warm."

Nodding, while gently setting his sacred pipe by his side, "She's even bossier than her mother was." Reaching over he opens the basket and removing a piece of chicken begins to eat.

Trying to suppress his smile, Stoney says in agreement, "And she usually gets her way."

Glancing at Stoney while he's eating, Black Eagle asks. "What is it?"

"What do you mean?"

Waving a piece of chicken, "Something's bothering you, what is it?"

The drumming has started in the arena. Listening to the drum, Stoney hesitates then. "It's really nothing. Dad and I were having another one of our little discussions at dinner, and I guess it just bothers me that he doesn't believe as we believe."

"You shouldn't let it bother you. Many people don't believe as we do and it doesn't matter. They don't have our knowledge of the spirits. They are not visited by the spirits as we are and have not had our visions."

Black Eagle picks up his sacred pipe and begins filling it with *(tsa-ru)* tobacco. "Always remember your father loves you with all his heart and would not hesitate to give his life for you. Remember this and always give him your love and respect, for he believes in what he is doing.

He believes money will make a better life for you and Morning Dove. His heart is good, and someday he will come to understand his real wealth comes from within. " Chuckling. "For now he is like an apple."

With a smile, "I know the saying. Redskin on the outside, white on the inside."

"But don't fault him, for true beliefs come from within, and I'm sure when your father was a young boy sitting around the campfires he heard the same stories you've heard. Because the Adawehis, (Dreamers) were telling stories of White Buffalo before the Great Buzzard flew across our country, making the Great Smokies. But he thought they were only stories. You knew it was history, our history."

"Tell me more about the White Buffalo."

Pausing while lighting his sacred pipe, Black Eagle takes a puff, while gazing at his grandson as if wanting to say more. Then slowly raises his pipe in an offering to the Great Spirit. Slowly exhales the smoke over his fire. While the drumming, continues in the background.

"I must have told you the story of White Buffalo a thousand times, no ten thousand times, since you were a little boy, and now you are a grown man." Pausing for a moment then continuing. "Before the Great Buzzard flew across our land to make the Great Smokies, before the Great Buzzard even learned to fly. Before the Great Spirit sent the White

Buffalo Calf Woman, to the Lakota, with our sacred pipe, the Great Spirit grew tired of the greed, famine and violence that were occurring throughout the land.

He choose an outstanding young brave, named him White Buffalo, and bestowed upon him the powers of the mightiest spirits, the power to call upon the powers of the White Buffalo.

Whose powers where so great, he could call down great bolts of lightning from the sky to strike terror and fear into the hearts of his enemies. He gave him the power to make the mightiest mountains tremble, and the power to open great chasms in mother earth. He gave him the power to talk to wild animals, and see through their eyes, but most important, he gave him the power to talk to and understand all people.

The Great Spirit told White Buffalo he was to use these powers wisely, that he was to put all the people before himself, and that he was to seek nothing for himself...

The Great Spirit sent him throughout the land, to bring peace to all the tribes, to all the people, the Crow. Delaware, Choctaw, Chickasaws, Creeks, Kickapoo, Sioux, Swanees, Mohawks, Apache, Navajo, Moskogee, Hopi, Seminoles, Chumash. To all people...

White Buffalo went forth throughout the land, spreading peace and helping people to understand each other's ways.

The tribes came together for Pow Wows, they danced together, sang together, celebrated together, worked together, and most importantly, they began to learn each other's ways.

The Great Spirit was happy... The tribes were happy, their harvests were good, their gatherings were good and their hunts were good. Everyone was happy.

Until one day, White Buffalo allowed himself to yield to temptation, and used his great powers in an act of greed in seeking something for himself...

The Great Spirit was hurt and offended, and stripped White Buffalo of his powers, telling him that someday the Great

Spirit would restore White Buffalo's powers. When he, the Great Spirit, decided White Buffalo was ready to accept these powers. With honor..."

As the drumming continues, Black Eagle raises his sacred pipe above the fire, as if offering his pipe to the Great Spirit.

Placing a few more branches on the fire while listening to the drums, Stoney asks. "I keep asking you and you keep telling me to have patience... But I have to ask again. When am I going to get my Indian name?"

"You know an Indian name can only be given by a Holy Man or a Chief."

"But you are a Holy Man, why don't you give me a name?

Hesitating then drawing on his pipe.

"Because you already have a name... You must have patience, you will learn it soon enough... Just be patient." Then, getting up, says, "Let's watch the dancers."

Stoney follows his grandfather out and stands beside him on the little knoll. As they watch, the dancers dressed in buckskin dresses and buckskin breeches dance to the beat of the mother drum. While sparks from the fire, still burning in the center of the dance arena, slowly drift into the night sky. A scene Stoney never tires of watching.

The sun has barely begun to peek over the mountain when the flap on the tepee opens and Stoney steps out, wearing only a buckskin loincloth, moccasins, a green cloth headband, and his medicine bag around his neck, to begin doing his stretching exercise. After warming up with his stretching exercise, he begins running, slowly at first and gradually increasing his pace.

As he is running through the meadow, his gaze falls upon a magnificent black and white paint stallion grazing on the other side of the meadow. He whistles, and the stallion raises his head and trots over to meet him in the middle of the meadow.

Stoney stops long enough to pat the beautiful stallion on the neck and say a few kind words to him, and then continues his running.

Crossing the meadow, Stoney enters the line of trees running along the stream, continuing up and over the hill.

An hour later Black Eagle is on the front porch of his log house sitting in his rocking chair, drinking a cup of coffee while gazing at the hill.

A smile pulls at the corner of his mouth, as Stoney appears running full out down the side of the hill. With the perspiration covering his muscles glistening in the morning sun; he increases his speed as he approaches the stream and suddenly turning, runs out on a huge rock over the crystal clear pool, and dives into the ice-cold water.

Surfacing, he swims across the pool and trots toward Black Eagle's log house. As he approaches the steps, Black Eagle tosses him a towel.

"Dry yourself and have a seat while I get some juice for you..."

When Black Eagle returns with the orange juice, Stoney is sitting on the steps, rubbing his hair with the towel. Setting the juice on the table, he asks. "Have you decided what you're going to do when you graduate next month?"

"Dad wants me to work with him and learn the oil business."

"That's not what I asked. I asked if you decided what you were going to do after you graduate."

Slowly shaking his head at his grandfather, "You always seem to know what I'm thinking... I guess I haven't really decided yet. I only know that I'm going to withdraw my name from the NFL draft... As much as I love to play football, I believe there has to be more to life than playing football." Pausing, then, "I've been taking a lot of pre-psychology classes these last few years and that really seems to interest me. Eventually I'd like to continue on to a Doctorate in psychology. But for now I think I'd like to just get out and meet some people, real people, our kind of people. I want to travel around the country and get to know people, how they live, how they think."

"Yes, I think you'd like that. But the only way you'll really get to know people is to be invisible, when you go among them."

Stoney stops drying his hair to look up at his grandfather... Standing, Black Eagle asks. "Are you hungry? Heck you're always hungry, and I think I've got enough ham and eggs in there to satisfy even your appetite."

"No thanks grandpa. I'd love to, but I promised Mom I'd have breakfast with them this morning"'

Sitting back in his chair, Black Eagle nods, "Well a promise is a promise. But be sure to thank your mother for the chicken, and tell her that I can take care of myself just fine and for her to stop worrying about me" Then with a smile and a little wink. "And tell her to put a little more salt on the chicken next time."

As Stoney climbs the mountain to get back to where he parked his truck, he stops to look back at his grandfathers beautiful little valley, as he wonders if he could actually ever leave.

John and Peggy are on the patio sitting under an umbrella at a marble topped table, drinking their orange juice, when Stoney arrives.

Peggy immediately asks. "How's Dad?

Stoney pauses as he gives her a kiss on her forehead, then pulling out a chair answers "He's fine. He said to tell you that he can take care of himself, just fine, and to thank you for the chicken... And to tell you to put a little more salt on the chicken next time."

Laughing, Peggy says, 'That sounds just like him, so I know he's alright." Pausing then asks, "What else did he say?

Glancing at his father, as he pours a glass of orange juice,

"Well, he told me that Dad loves me, but I already knew that."

A little embarrassed while trying not to show it, John drinks some juice and tries to change the subject.

"I've invited a few of my business associates over next Saturday to go hunting. Would you like to join us?"

Shocked, Stoney can't believe what he's just heard.

"I can't believe this. You've never allowed anyone to hunt on the Rainbolt."

"I know but there's really a little more to it than just a hunting trip.

We've been talking about starting a mining operation in Granite Peaks and they wanted to get a look at it..."

"Granite Peaks is one of the last few remaining pristine areas in the entire State. ' Shaking his head, "I can't believe you would ever allow anyone in there to hunt, much less start a mining operation in there."

"We talked about that, they said they'll guarantee to put it back in its natural state when they're through."

Shaking his head, "I really don't think you believe that, Dad. It took someone, a lot more powerful than they are, millions of years to create Granite Peaks. Granite mining is a form of strip mining with extensive blasting, huge bulldozers, and mammoth trucks. They'll just tear the mountains down, and for them to claim they could put it back together in it's natural state after they've torn it down is next to blasphemous." Pausing, then. "I'm sorry Dad, I know you're only doing what you think is best, so I won't say anymore about it... But I can't have anything to do with it either." Slowly, shaking his head, Stoney stands. "I think I just lost my appetite, so if you'll excuse me, I think I'll change my clothes and take a ride."

3

Granite Peaks

As Stoney is walking toward the house, sounding concerned, Peggy asks. "Where are you going?"

"Granite Peaks."

Parking his truck near the base of Granite Peaks, in a grove of cottonwood trees, Stoney sits for a few minutes. Gazing at the beauty of these mountains of solid granite, glowing with the reflection of the morning sun in such a manner Stoney has never noticed before.

Getting out of his truck, he stands absorbing the indescribable rugged beauty of these magnificent mountains. Thinking some million or so years ago a powerful force literally pushed these massive granite stones from the center of the earth. Upward until they formed these majestic mountains, then covered them with towering pines and crowned them with a crown of glistening white snow.

Not really knowing why he came or what he is going to do now that he is here. Only knowing he felt compelled to come. Almost as if the mountains were drawing him to them, when suddenly he feels he must climb these magnificent towering mountains.

Wearing only buckskin breeches, his medicine bag, moccasins and a bowie knife on his belt, Stoney ties a bright green cloth band around his forehead.

Then turning and facing the mountains he feels calm, cleansing determination as he starts up the mountain.

He barely reaches the timberline, when he notices a little gray fox seemingly unafraid, watching him as he passes within feet of the curious little fox.

Continuing on, he crosses a little clearing where several deer are drinking from a gentle stream. They raise their heads to watch as he passes, undisturbed they continue their drinking.

As the terrain gets steeper and the climbing more difficult, perspiration on his chest and back begins to glisten in the sunlight as he climbs ever higher. Suddenly feeling an unexplained urgency, Stoney increases his pace.

Wiping his brow, his fatigue seemingly goes unnoticed as he continues to climb. Pausing a few minutes later to gaze at the natural beauty surrounding him, Stoney wonders how anyone could ever doubt such beauty could possibly be created by anything except, our Creator. His entire body feels warm and good as he imagines he can feel the presence of our supreme being, as he, gazes at the sparkling white fluffy clouds, floating haphazardly, through a soft blue sky above the gently rolling emerald green hills. The shaded valleys of the Rainbolt ranch are dotted with contented grazing cattle far below. His attention is suddenly drawn to a black bear and her cub slowly moving through the trees just down the mountain.

Turning, Stoney continues his climb until he comes to an almost solid vertical wall of shimmering granite, with only a few cracks and fissures in its surface. Having previously made many such free solo climbs without benefit of safety ropes or hardware, Stoney begins ascending the sheer face of this 200-foot granite wall without hesitation, hand over hand, using only his toes, fingertips, and nerve.

He enjoys his climb, as muscles in his shoulders and arms are first warming then almost burning as he approaches the top of the sheer granite wall.

Hearing a low menacing growl coming from just over the ledge, he increases his effort.

Finally able to pull himself up on the narrow ledge, he confronts a large puma, standing less than twenty feet away.

The big cat is crouching, its head lowered, watching Stoney's every move with its bright glowing yellow eyes, its mouth slightly open exposing its sparkling white teeth, emitting a deep low growl, with its ears pinned back flat against its skull, its tail moving slowly back and forth as if ready to spring.

Stoney stands and faces the huge cat as it growls louder. Then suddenly turning, the big cat rushes across the narrow ledge leaping on overhanging rocks, where it disappears down a small, almost invisible trail.

Turning, Stoney absorbs the magnificent panoramic view of the beautiful valley, stretching out far below.

When suddenly he is distracted by the screeching of an eagle and, looking further up the cliff, he watches as an eagle feeds her eaglets. Hearing another louder screeching, his gaze is directed to another even larger eagle, soaring directly over his head. He watches in amazement as the eagle suddenly dives, pulling out of his dive within mere feet of where he is standing, and watches as the eagle begins soaring in circles not a hundred feet above his head. As he watches, he notices a small dark spot seemingly drifting back and forth as if on a soft breeze and then suddenly begins to spiral down to fall at his feet, an eagle feather.

Picking the eagle feather up, he suddenly feels a warm sense of power slowly engulfing his entire body, and something telling him he must not allow the destruction of these mountains. Then unexplainably, Stoney steps to the very edge of the granite cliff. Holding the eagle feather firmly between his thumb and forefinger, throwing his closed fists, high in the air and rising on his toes, throws his head back and shouts as loud as he can. "Yaaaaaaaaaaaaaaaaaaaaaaaaaa."

That evening Stoney is sitting around the fire explaining to Black Eagle how he felt compelled to climb Granite Peaks.

"I don't even know why I went there; I only know I felt drawn to the mountains. When I got there, I was almost mesmerized by their beauty, as they appeared to be glowing in the sunlight.

When suddenly, I felt compelled to climb the mountains, and when I climbed the granite cliff and confronted the puma he seemed to know, I belonged there." Slowly shaking his head, then continuing, "It seemed as if neither, the fox, the deer, the bear, or even the puma were afraid of me. When I saw how unafraid the animals were. I knew what dad and his friends were planning would be a slaughter, not a hunting trip.

Then, when the eagle feather drifted down and fell at my feet and I picked it up, a warm power seemed to flow over me. Something was telling me that I must not allow Granite Peaks to be destroyed, nor allow the slaughter of these creatures."

Shaking his head, "But I told my father I would not say anymore to him about their mining operation. So what am I to do grandfather? I know I must do something, but I don't know what I can do. Help me grandfather."

Lighting his sacred pipe from the burning embers, Black Eagle makes the pipe offering to the four directions, then looking at his grandson. "I have been helping and advising you since you were merely a baby, and I shall always be by your side to offer guidance and help whenever you need it.

However, you have received the sign from the Great Spirit, telling you that you are ready to do what ever he may ask of you… I have taught you many things over the years, one of which was the importance of patience… Have patience now and the Great Spirit will show you the way..." Pausing while puffing on his sacred pipe, then, "I have known for many years this day would come.

And as of this day, your powers exceed even my own. They exceed every power ever imagined by man.

Learn these powers; learn them well, learn them as well as you know yourself... Listen to the Great Spirit and use these powers wisely...

You have always asked what your Indian name was and I could not tell you, as the time for you to know had not yet come. Now I can tell you, your name has been given to you, not by me, but by the greatest of all Holy Men, the Great Spirit..." Pause   "You are...White Buffalo."
Suddenly, the little fire between them flares up as the beat of the drum increases in tempo.

Black Eagle continues. "When you go among the people, you are not to tell them your name. They will know only when the Great Spirit wishes them to know.

Go among them with an open mind, an open heart, and a helping hand. Listen to them, listen to their needs, and listen to the Great Spirit, he will guide you."

Stunned at what he has heard. Stoney gasps, "No grandfather, this can't be true. I'm not worthy of such powers."

"The Great Spirit has been training for this quest since before you were five years old, and I have merely been directing you in your training. The Great Spirit has been your instructor.
If he did not think you were worthy of doing what he asks of you, he would not have sent his eagle feather to you or asked you to preserve either his creatures or his mountains."

"But how? I have told my father I would not say anymore to him about it, and I don't know what I can do to stop them. I don't know what anyone can do."

"But this is only Sunday and they are not going to Granite Peaks to hunt until Saturday. That gives you six days to think upon it. And there are some who say creation only took the Great Spirit six days to accomplish then he rested on the seventh.

But above all else, listen to the Great Spirit, he will give you guidance." And with a smile, "Then maybe we too can rest on the seventh."

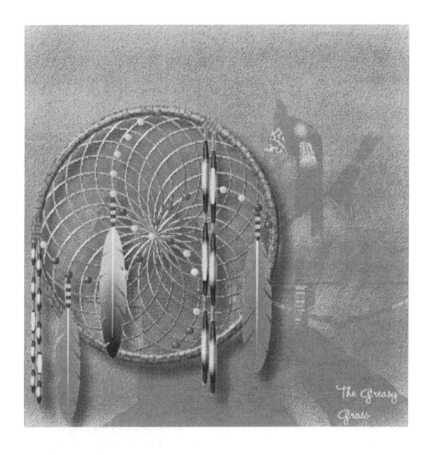

As Traditional People, we believe we belong to Mother Earth, she does not belong to us.

4

The Vision

The University of Oklahoma is known world wide for its research and training in the field of Geology. Taking full advantage of this wealth of knowledge, Stoney spends every free hour he can possibly spare away from his regular studies, in the school library researching granite and the various methods of its mining.

The more he reads the more he knows he must not allow it to happen in the Granite Peaks.

He spends the evenings consulting with Black Eagle and the days seem to be rushing by, still he finds no answer to his dilemma.

Exhausted after almost a grueling week of thirteen and fourteen hour days at school studying for his finals, coupled with the countless hours he's spent in the library, researching anything he could find on the subject of granite mining, Stoney parks his pickup truck at the end of the road above Black Eagle Valley. Mentally exhausted and almost too tired to get out of his truck, he turns to watch the sun as it sets behind the Granite Peaks Mountains while thinking how beautiful they are. When suddenly, he realizes the scene before his eyes is changing. Instead of the sunset, he is watching a great storm gather over Granite Peaks with some of the blackest storm clouds he has ever seen. Then suddenly great bolts of lightning explode one after another, out of the black ominous looking clouds, flashing across the sky in their race for the mountains. Thunder so loud it is almost deafening as it rolls across the countryside, as torrents of rain begin pouring down on the Granite Peaks.

Then suddenly everything is calm and once again, he is watching the beautiful sunset as the sun slowly sets behind the Granite Peaks.

Stoney is explaining to Black Eagle what he saw in his vision. "I could actually see the lightning one after another flashing across the sky. I could hear the thunder rolling through the valley and see the rain falling in torrents, and then suddenly it was gone."

Nodding, "Yes, it was truly a vision. The Great Spirit has spoken; he has told you what you must do."

Shaking his head, "But how, how am I supposed to make a storm, especially a storm such as I saw in my vision?

"The great Spirit will show you the way."

"But my father will be there and the storm I saw was truly horrendous."

"The Great Spirit would not allow harm to come to your father or anyone else. That is not his way."

"No I don't believe he would." Looking into the fire and thinking for a moment, then in a doubtful tone, "This is crazy grandfather, I don't know if I'm worthy enough to do what he's asking."

"He must think you are or he wouldn't ask."

Shaking his head, "I can't sleep, I lay awake and think about everything that's happened in these last few days. Now mom is even starting to ask questions. She says I'm looking tired, and I keep telling her that getting ready for finals is tough.

Which in itself is the truth, I just don't tell her the rest of it, and I find that extremely difficult because I can't ever remember not being able to confide in her."

"Yes, I'm sure that must be most difficult for you. But there will come a time in the not so distant future when both your mother and father will learn everything." Pausing, then continuing, "I know that will make both of them extremely proud of the son they have raised. Now I would suggest you go home, and after you do your studying try to get some sleep, for tomorrow night we will be honored with many prayer dancers."

Late Friday afternoon, Stoney turns in the ranch parking area as his father and two ranch hands are loading tents and camping gear into three of the ranch jeeps. Parking his truck and carrying an arm full of books, he walks over to his father.

Nodding toward the jeeps, "This looks more like the invasion of Normandy than a hunting trip."

"Yeah I guess it does, and I know it must look a little ridiculous. However, I'm only trying to make these guys as comfortable as possible." Shaking his head, "I don't think any of them could even find the executive bathroom if they didn't have executive secretaries to tell them where it was.
I don't think any of them have the slightest idea what they're getting into, because none of them has ever gone hunting before." Chuckling, John continues, "I can't wait to see the expression on their face when one of them asks me where the rest room is, and I tell them, behind that tree."

Laughing, "You don't sound like you're enjoying this."

Slowly shaking his head, "I'm really not, and I keep asking myself when I'm ever going to learn to keep my big mouth shut."

Smiling from ear to ear, "Thanks Dad, that makes me feel better, knowing you're not enjoying your hunting trip."

John laughs. "Yeah well that's a terrible thing to say to your father, but I know what you mean, so I'll let you get away with it, if you promise to be here when we get back I'd like them to meet my son."

"Looking at the open jeeps, Stoney smiles. "I promise Dad, I'll be here. In fact I wouldn't miss it for the world. I'm just sorry I can't go with you, but you know I don't believe in hunting for sport. Even the wolf and the Puma don't kill for sport."

"I know, and I want you to know; I realize I shouldn't have allowed this to happen."

Nodding in understanding, "Now that we're through with all this mutual admiration stuff, let's go see what Mom's made for dinner."

"You got that right, Mom won't let that cook do anything around here and when I mentioned to her I was thinking about letting him go, she told me I couldn't do that because he needed the job."

Shaking his head and muttering to himself, John leads the way in.

Peggy is setting the table when John and Stoney walk in, immediately handing the silverware to Stoney,

"I know you're in a hurry to get to your grandfather's this evening, so if you'll finish setting the table, I'll start serving dinner."

As Stoney finishes setting the table, John takes a seat.

"Oh, you got a call from Dallas today; they didn't say what they wanted. They just said they'd call back. But, I'll bet they want you to play for the Cowboys."

"It would be a real honor to play for any team like the Cowboys, but I don't think that's what I want to do with my life."

Peggy is all smiles as she sets a big plate of roast beef in front of Stoney. "Thank goodness! I never did like you playing that game. I was always afraid you were going to get hurt."

"You know you can always come to work with me, and I'd be happy to make you a full partner."

"Thanks Dad, that's a great offer and I may very likely take you up on it down the line, but I don't think I'm quite ready for it just yet. I've been thinking I might like to do some traveling first."

"Traveling is a great idea and you can learn a lot about people that way. Maybe you should take six months or even a year and travel around the world." John says in agreement.

"I wasn't really thinking about going around the world, I thought I'd like to see a little more of our country first. I thought I'd just go down the road from town to town doing a little roping and bull riding."

Sounding shocked, "You mean rodeos? That's more dangerous than playing football." Peggy says.

"Now honey, don't get upset, you know Stoney's no greenhorn when it comes to rodeos, he's the best there is around here."

"I know, but I'll still worry about him."

"Of course you will and so will I, but we both know he can and will take care of himself."

"Thanks Dad, but it's not definite yet, it's just something I'm considering because it would give me the opportunity to meet, work with and get to know real everyday kind of people."

John is beginning to bristle. "You mean people who don't have a ranch like the Rainbolt sitting on one of the biggest pools of oil in the country?"

"No Dad, that's not what I meant. I know you have worked hard to get where you are today, and I love and respect you for all you've done. But you and Mom didn't always have money. Grandpa told me he remembers when you guys didn't know how you were going to make the next mortgage or car payment. He told me there were times when you didn't even have a car to make a payment on. He also told me how through all that, your love and faith in each other never wavered. Those are the kind of people I want to meet and get to know, people just like you and mom."

John reaches across the table to take Peggy's hand. "It kind of looks like we have a son we can be proud of, in more ways than we ever imagined."

Than turning back to Stoney,   "Whatever you decide to do, you can count on our support."

Squeezing John's hand, Peggy says, "That's true, but I'm still going to worry about him."

"Thanks, I knew I could count on you both, but I better hurry or grandpa's going to be wondering what happened to me."

"Just relax and finish your dinner, while I fix a plate for him."

"And I've got some tobacco for him." John says.

"Thanks dad, I know he'll appreciate it." Than hesitantly, "When will the great white hunters be arriving?"

"I told them to be here by 2:30 or 3:00 at the latest, so we would have time to get there and hike into Granite Peaks well before sunup. And don't forget, you promised to be here when we got back."

Smiling, "You can count on it Dad."

Setting a basket on the table, Peggy reminds him, "Don't forget to tell him to eat this while it's hot."

After parking his truck, Stoney takes the basket and, walking to the edge of the cliff, looks down into Black Eagle's valley where he sees more activity than usual. As he crosses the stream he sees Black Eagle in the dance arena, blessing and purifying it for this evening's ceremonial dances.

Not wanting to disturb him, Stoney goes directly to the tepee to change his clothes and wait for his grandfather.

When Black Eagle enters the tepee, Stoney rises and waits until his grandfather takes his seat by the fire. Then indicating the basket, says, "Morning Dove sent you some dinner and you know she's going to ask, so you better eat it while it's hot." Motioning toward the basket, "And dad sent some tobacco for you."

Black Eagle opens the basket and removing the tobacco examines it, and nodding his head in approval sets it aside. Then taking a plate out, uncovers it and begins eating, and between mouthfuls says, "It's almost as good as her mother used to make." Then after another mouthful. "Be sure to thank your father for the tobacco *(Tsa-ru)."*   .

"Are the dancers going to be here soon?"

As Black Eagle looks up from his plate, "Some of them are already here, others will be here shortly, and I asked for four drummers to drum and sing for us tonight." Then nodding toward Stoney, "I can see you're nervous… Relax, there's nothing to be nervous about." Then setting his plate aside he picks up his sacred pipe and begins filling it with tobacco. "Just relax and clear your mind, of everything except your quest."

Stoney is wearing a long sleeve deerskin shirt decorated with brightly colored beads, and with fringe hanging from his shoulders and sleeves. Holding his eagle feather in both hands and sitting up straight while gazing into the fire, he slowly raises the feather above the fire and begins chanting.

As the drumming commences, Black Eagle rises and goes to the ceremonial arena to perform a purification ritual with burning sage and sweet grass, while chanting prayers over each dancer before they enter the sacred arena.

Four drummers, two sitting on each side of a big mother drum, suspended above the ground in a cradle of rawhide decorated with eagle feathers, beat a steady rhythm for the dancers. They enter the arena from the east and begin dancing around the fire in a clockwise direction, while sparks from the fire slowly drift into the night sky.

The drum beats; always steady as if it were the beat of our mother earth's heart. Sometimes slow, sometimes fast, sometimes slow and gradually increasing its tempo, then suddenly stopping for a few beats, then beginning again.

The head dancer, wearing a brightly colored turban and carrying a feather decorated buffalo shield, leads a score of dancers dressed in traditional dress. Some carrying tortuous shell or gourd rattles as they chant their prayers, while they dance to the tempo of the drum. Without missing a beat, they dance hour after hour, with their minds on their ancestors and our Creator, seemingly never to tire.

Black Eagle has returned to the tepee, sitting by the fire smoking his sacred pipe, he quietly begins chanting prayers. While Stoney, holding the eagle feather slightly above the flames, gazes into the fire, which can be seen reflected in the thin layer of perspiration covering his forehead and face...

Looking into the fire, Stoney sees an almost transparent image of Granite Peak Mountains, with menacing black clouds and flashing bolts of lightning above the mountains. Finally, Stoney slowly lowers his arms and relaxes in an almost exhausted condition.

Black Eagle, setting his sacred pipe aside, rises and with Stoney following, they exit the tepee and slowly walk to the dance arena. Where they stand side by side, each engrossed in their own thoughts, watching the dancers.

Until Black Eagle gives a slight almost un-noticeable nod and, as if they were one, both drummers and dancers immediately stop. As they leave the arena, Black Eagle and Stoney thank them for their efforts.

The firewatcher adds a few more logs to the fire, then he too departs.

Black Eagle and Stoney turn and slowly walk around the arena, then under the cottonwoods and along the stream toward the pool.

Black Eagle asks. "Are you still feeling uneasy?"

"Are you kidding? This is all I've been able to think about for days and, to be truthful, it scares me."

"If it didn't scare you, I'd worry."

"I guess what really scares me is, I don't know if I'm worthy of such a trust."

"As I've told you, if you were not worthy of such trust, the Great Spirit would not have put his trust in you."

"What if I make a mistake?"

As they reach a bend in the stream, they turn and follow its bank and Black Eagle answers. "Listen to the Great Spirit and you won't make mistakes."

"But if I failed, I don't think I could face any of you ever again."

Looking at his grandson, "You should never feel that way... We love you, and nothing you could ever do would change that."

"But I could fail."

"I've known you your entire life, and I've never known you to accept failure. And you will not allow yourself to fail in this."

Slowly shaking his head, "I only wish I had your confidence."

"Remember when you were in high school, when you played your first game of football? I remember you telling me how afraid you were, standing out there in the middle of the field waiting for the kickoff. Hearing the bands playing and everyone in the stadium yelling, knowing the whole school was watching.

You told me how afraid you were of making a mistake... However, when the kickoff came and you made that first contact, you forgot about being afraid. You forgot about everyone in the stands and played the game by instinct, giving it everything you had...

That's the way you've played all your games, and that's what you have to do here... Play by instinct and give it all you've got. That's all anyone, even the Great Spirit, can ask."

"But this isn't a football game and I wasn't expecting anything like this, this involves people's lives, real people.

And it's all been so sudden, and I wasn't even asked if I wanted to play. I was told the Great Spirit has given the ball to me and now I'm supposed to run with it... And I guess what I'm trying to say, it just comes down to the fact that I'm scared, really scared."

"I know you're scared and you're right, you weren't asked, you were chosen before you were even born. You were chosen, just as I was chosen to guide and teach you everything I knew. Everything except one thing, that being what you were chosen for. However you should know that you don't have to do this. The decision is still yours to make. And should you decide not to do what is asked of you, it will never be mentioned again.

Now I will leave you alone to consider your decision, with clear eyes..."

Black Eagle turns and walks toward his log house, while Stoney stands watching his grandfather walk away. Then turning himself, he continues to walk along the stream to the pool where he sits on one of the large stones overlooking the pool.

The reflection of the full moon shining on the surface of the pool is suddenly shattered as a fish jumps, causing ripples in the pool. Watching these ripples, he wonders what rippling effect this development in his life will cause. He sits there for hours, thinking about his family that he loves so deeply. Thinking about what he would be giving up, should he accept what he has been asked. His thoughts interrupted only occasionally by the lonely hoot of an owl or the far off yipping of coyotes.

Shortly before dawn, Stoney rises and slowly walks to the tepee.

5

The Hunters

The jeeps bounce along the seldom-used trail approaching Granite Peaks Mountains, their headlights illuminating an occasional rabbit. They stop at the cottonwoods near the base of the Mountains. The four hunters and two ranch hands climb out and begin unloading their gear from the jeeps.

John is giving last minute instructions to one of the ranch hands.

"We better not take the jeeps any further; it would only scare the game... We'll hike in from here. You and Jim can set up camp under those cottonwoods. I know these guys are going to be worn out when we get back, and hot coffee and a little breakfast should do wonders for them."

Bob a Native American, forties, is wearing weathered jeans, an old western hat, well worn boots, and his medicine bag hanging around his neck outside his sun bleached western shirt.

"No problem boss, we'll have everything ready for a nice hot breakfast when you get back." Then lowering his voice, "Just be careful out there John. These guys don't much look like they know what their doing. And if it was me out there with them, I'd be worrying if they were carrying those loaded guns around me."

Chuckling, "I was thinking the same thing." John says, as he motions toward the hunters and asks, "Did you ever see anything like this before?"

John and Bob turn to look at the hunters. Williams, wearing a bright neon orange hat and a brand new pair of Ostrich skin boots, is trying to be careful where he steps and, evidently wanting to keep them shined, stops every fourth or fifth step and raises one of the boots and tries to polish it on the back of the opposite calf.

"He said those boots cost him sixteen hundred dollars... I can't help wondering what they're going to look like after this hunting trip. And look at that ammunition belt he's wearing around his waist, it looks like he's expecting to meet Poncho Villa out here.

And David over there, wearing that brand new shooting jacket with those nice fancy leather patches on his shoulder and elbows. He looks like he's ready for a day of skeet shooting at the country club." Pausing then, John continues as he nudges Bob with his elbow, "The one over there looking down the barrel of that new forty-seven hundred dollar rifle. Which I sure hope isn't loaded, he must think he's going after elephants with that rifle. And Phil, the little round guy over their wearing that bright orange vest has a 20x scope on that rifle of his, I guess he doesn't want to get too close to anything he decides to shoot at, and look at the size of that canteen he's carrying around his waist, it must weigh twenty pounds. Imagine carrying that up these mountain. At least he won't get lost; he brought a two-dollar compass with him. I just hope he doesn't have to depend on it." Then slowly shaking his head, "Well I guess I better stop putting it off and get this circus on the road."

Smiling, Bob says, "I'd like to say, I wish I was going with you, but I'm sorry boss, I can't lie. All I can say is good luck... And be careful."

John nods his head at Bob in agreement and calls out, "Alright, let's get going… If we want to get back in those mountains before the sun comes up, we better get a move on."

With the full moon lighting their way, the hunters begin their hike into the mountains, and it is a circus indeed. With William muttering to himself every time he scuffs his boots on a rock or tree root. Phil stopping every ten minutes to either check his compass or drink from the canteen that's already beginning to cause his belt and pants to slip below his round belly.

William muttering almost to himself, "Darn, I'm going to ruin these pretty boots."

Stopping again, this time to pull his pants back up, Phil tells him, "You'll be glad you wore those boots, if you step on a snake."

"Snake!… Are there snakes around here?"

"Of course there are and snakes are nocturnal, that means they're out at night."

"I know what nocturnal means, but no one told me anything about snakes being around here. If they had, I would have brought a snake bite kit."

Hearing this, John decides he's going to liven things up and have a little fun with these guys. "If I were you, I wouldn't be worrying about no little snakes; I'd worry more about the bears. You only have to worry about snakes if you step on them, but bears, they are something else. They're just plain ornery and they'll come charging out from behind a tree, a bush or a rock like an express train without any warning at all, and you don't even have to step on them."

Phil, looking a little nervous, takes his rifle off his shoulder and holds it at ready as he tries to peer into the darkness, and every once in awhile tries to peer through the scope. While still trying to juggle his canteen and compass, and keep his pants up all at the same time.

David raises his rifle across his chest and puts his finger on the trigger, and John begins to wonder if he really should have started all this.

William, forgetting about snakes and scuffing his boots takes a firmer grip on his rifle and asks, "Don't bears sleep this time of the year?"

"No, they hibernate in the winter and, when they wake up, usually around this time of the year, they're hungry because they've gone without eating for so long."

William takes an even firmer grip on his rifle...

Everyone looks worried when David asks. "Is it getting darker or am I just imagining it?"

John has been thinking the same thing. "No I don't think it's your imagination. When we left the jeeps the full moon was out, bright enough to almost read by. But now, there are some very black ominous looking clouds over us."

William trying to be optimistic, "Maybe it gets darker before it gets light."

Chuckling to himself, John says,. "I think your confusing that with the saying. It's always darkest before the storm, and in that you may just be right. Because it sure looks like we're going to be in for a good one. We might just be in for one of our spring thunder storms, you can even feel the high humidity in the air."

Still trying to be optimistic, William says, "Storm, what storm? I didn't hear anything about a storm; no one said anything about a storm to me."

Looking at the dark clouds Phil shrugs his shoulders. "It can't rain, I watched Channel 3 News last night and they didn't say anything about a storm"

"I sure hope you're right; I wouldn't want to get these boots wet"

Squinting at his compass, Phil says. "But it's getting so dark; I can't even see my compass anymore."

John's shaking his head. "Well if we're going to get back in these mountains before sunup we better get a move on, we've come less than 2 miles since we left the jeeps."
The hunters pick up their pace.

It's almost sunup when the flap on the tepee opens and Stoney steps out wearing his medicine bag a loincloth, moccasins, and a bright white cloth band wrapped around his forehead, with the eagle feather hanging over his right shoulder.

After doing a few warm up exercises, he begins running across the meadow. The big stallion looks up, but Stoney doesn't stop to either whistle or pet him. He continues running across the meadow and through the trees and through the stream.

By the time he approaches the steep hill his body is covered with perspiration. Still he pushes on, every muscle in his body straining as he runs faster and faster up the hill until he finally reaches the summit. Turning toward Granite Peaks he sees the sun just beginning to peek over the highest mountain.

Running to the edge of the cliff and throwing his head back, with his face towards the sky and stretching both arms in the air with closed fists, screams into the crisp morning air. "Yaaaaaaaaaaaaaaaaaaaaaaa!"

Then, looking toward Granite Peaks, he sees lightning bolt after lightning bolt explode from the black menacing clouds that have gathered over Granite Peaks. Lighting the night sky in their dash to those mighty mountains, and almost immediately he hears an almost continuous roll of slow rumbling thunder rolling through the entire valley, seeming to shake the very earth he's standing on.

Knowing Granite Peaks and all its creatures are safe, at least for now, he smiles as he turns and resumes his running.

The beauty of life is found in the adventure of every day.
(Unknown)

6

Storm over Granite Peaks

Having hurried into the mountains, the hunters are peering into the darkness, straining to see <u>anything</u> they can shoot at Their rifles cradled in their arms, they anxiously await the first light of day, when suddenly a huge bolt of lightning explodes, directly, over their heads, tearing the night sky apart in an almost blinding flash of brightness. Followed immediately by a clap of thunder so loud two of the hunters drop their rifles and clap their hands over their ears.

Then suddenly the heavens are ripped apart as a deluge of rain pours down, drenching them all in a matter of seconds. Lightning bolt after lightning bolt flashes through the sky and through the mountains passes, followed by thunder so loud it seems to ricochet from one canyon wall to another. The torrential rain continues to pour down on the hunters, turning the soil under their feet to a slick sticky mud.

Terrified, William begins shouting. "I knew it, I knew it… We're going to be killed. We're all going to be killed"

Trying to calm him, John grabs his shoulder and has to shout to be heard above the rolling roar of thunder. "Calm down… We're not going to get killed, just a little wet."

"No, we're going to get killed… Haven't you ever heard of a flash flood? We're going to be killed in a flash flood."

Williams's outburst spooks the others; Phil and David look around as if expecting to see a twenty-foot high wall of white water crashing down through the canyons.

John tries again." It's probably just a thunder shower and will probably be over in a few minutes ".   Then, thinking this is his chance to get these guys out of here, continues, "But maybe we should start back to camp where we can at least get dried out."

Little round Phil seconds the motion. "That's a good idea John, let's get out of here." Suddenly turning, Phil begins to run down a small muddy slick slope, as the weight of his canteen pulls his pants down around his knees. Causing him to take a fall and slide a few feet on his belly in the soft slimy mud, covering his face and bright orange vest with a thick layer of mud, not to mention filling his pants with gobs of the slimy mud.

Struggling to his knees, while trying to pull his pants up with his muddy hands Phil whines, "Oh my god, Oh my god, look at me, I'm covered with mud."

William, boots covered with mud, steps forward to help Phil to his feet, only to have Phil suddenly screech again. "Oh my god, Oh my god, look what you've done, you stepped on my compass. You broke my compass... Now we're lost, we'll never get out of here."

Picking up Phil's rifle, while thinking it would probably be safer for everyone if he carried it himself, John slings it over his shoulder and says, "No we're not lost and we won't get lost. All we have to do is go down this canyon and we'll come out by the jeeps."

David joins in. "Yeah I know the way, just follow me." Not waiting for anyone, David turns and rushes down the canyon, as the lightning and thunder continue to explode throughout the canyons. While John is thinking, I sure hope David knows where he's going.

Ignoring his mud covered boots and holding his rifle in his left hand, William reaches out and, taking Phil's mud soaked arm, helps him to his feet, saying. "Now just follow David and you won't get lost and I'll be right behind you. But for god's sake, get rid of that canteen and keep your pants up."

Nodding his mud soaked head; Phil discards his canteen and broken compass. Then, while holding his pants up with both hands, awkwardly stumbles down the canyon after David with William following and John taking up the rear.

As our disheartened hunting party treks down the canyon, the rain, as if it were possible, seems to come down even harder. The lightning strikes seem to be coming closer and closer to the hunters in their headlong rush out of the mountains.

Feeling as if he's leading a group of settlers through Donner's Pass, David comes to a little gully about 10 to 12 feet deep. He notices a small game trail angling down the gully to the right and is about to start that way, when an extremely ice-cold wind strikes him from the rear raising the collar of his new jacket, causing him, to suddenly decide the direct route is the most expedient. Stepping to the edge of the gully, David decides the slope doesn't appear too steep. But as he takes that first step over the edge, he finds out how wrong he is, when his mud caked feet shoot out from under him and he lands on his backside. Sliding down the already saturated slope in about a foot of slimy mud, David drops his forty-seven hundred dollar rifle. While trying in vain to grab any little bush he comes near, only to have them slip through his mud slick hands. When he reaches the bottom of the gully he finds he's sitting in a 2 foot deep river of slowly moving slimy mud. Struggling to his feet, he stumbles over his brand new mud covered rifle, causing him to fall headfirst in the river of slimy mud.

Following a little ways behind David, all Phil sees is David sit rather awkwardly in the mud and slide down the embankment. And thinking, that looks easy enough, sits down on the slope and slides down like a little kid sliding down a snow bank.

Seeing what Phil is about to do, William rushes forward to stop him and in reaching out to grab Phil's shoulder, steps too close to the embankment which gives way, and William finds himself sliding down the slope head first.

Watching all this unfold, John can't believe what he's seeing. His first concern is for their safety, and he cautiously hurries to the embankment and peers over its edge, but seeing three of the States top executives stumbling around in that river of mud is too much for him. He begins to laugh and suddenly afraid they'll hear him, clamps his hand over his mouth.

Williams covered in mud, looks up the embankment at John and cupping his muddy hands to his mouth, calls out against the wind and rain. "You better hurry John, it's getting worse."

Raising his arm, as if to urge them on John calls back. "Go ahead, I'll catch up."

John cannot believe what he is seeing as he watches these three executives, covered in mud from head to foot, stumble their way down the canyon. John lets it go and, bending over in laughter, leans back against a pine tree and slowly sinks to the ground in a fit of uncontrollable laughter. While he lets the clear cool rainwater run down his face and is laughing when an extremely bright lightning bolt flashes through the mountains. Lighting the entire mountain range as if it were mid-day, giving John his first clear view, of these magnificent mountains, with their crown of glistening white snow.

"Stoney's right, this is too beautiful to allow anyone to destroy." John says to himself in a soft voice.

Getting to his feet, he walks over to the embankment and carefully walks down the little game trail to the mud river where he finds a fallen tree trunk crossing the river of mud.

In a matter of minutes, he has caught up with his mud-covered hunters.

The rain begins to slacken as they reach the little camp Bob and Jim has set up by the cottonwoods. A small tent and a slightly larger shelter, with a pot of coffee and skillets filled with sizzling ham are on a small campfire.

Both Bob and Jim are shocked, and can only stand with their mouths open while shaking their heads in amazement. Not knowing what to say, they stand in silence as they watch the mud covered hunters straggle into camp. John while wet, is relatively free of mud except what mud is on his boots. However, the other three are covered from head to toe in a thick layer of solid mud.

Avoiding the obvious question, he is dying to ask, Bob is finally able to stammer out. "When the rain started, we figured you'd be coming back pretty soon, so breakfast is almost ready and there's plenty of hot coffee,"

Wiping mud from his face, William flicks the mud on the ground and whines. "I don't want coffee; I just want to go home."

This is echoed by Phil and David.

John turns to Bob and Jim, nodding toward the mud covered hunters, "I should probably get these guys home where they can get cleaned up. You and Jim can enjoy the hot coffee and breakfast while you wait for the rain to stop. Then you can break camp and haul the gear back to the ranch." Shaking his head, while unable to suppress a little smile, "Just promise you'll never ask me what happened out there, because you'd never believe it".

John herds the three muddy hunters into one of the jeeps, and heads for home along the now muddy trail.

Black Eagle is rocking back and forth in his rocking chair as he watches the hill waiting for Stoney to appear. A slight

smile appears on his face when he sees Stoney running down
the mountain and diving into the ice cold pool.
A short time later Stoney comes trotting up to the log house.
Black Eagle throws him a towel.

"It looks like they may be getting a little rain up Granite
Peaks way."

Glancing toward Granite Peaks while continuing to dry off,
"Yeah, it kind of looks that way."

"You don't suppose anyone got wet do you?"

"Maybe a little."

Nodding, then, "Have a seat when you're through drying
and have some juice."

Draping the towel over the handrail Stoney picks up the
juice. "Thanks."

"Hungry?"

"Hungry as a bear, but I want to give Roamer a little
exercise first... With everything going on, I seem to have been
ignoring him lately."

"Go ahead. I'll put breakfast on and it'll be ready when
you're through."

"Thanks grandpa, I won't be too long."
Stepping off the porch and looking toward the pasture, Stoney
whistles. Hearing his whistle, the big stallion raises his head
and begins trotting to Stoney.

Stoney pats and rubs his neck, while quietly talking to the
big horse, then taking some mane in his left hand he swings up
on Roamer's back. Sensing the slight pressure of Stoney's legs
and heels, Roamer begins to move forward, and taking his
cues from Stoney's legs, heels, and shifting weight, begins a
series of figure eights and circles, both to the right and left
without hesitation or missing a lead change. Then breaking out
in a lope, and increasing speed as they approach the stream,
almost effortlessly with rider and horse as one, they leap the
stream. Then race up the hill to its summit, where Roamer
rears up and spins on his rear legs.

Starting back down the hill at a more leisurely pace until reaching the pool where Roamer walks out in the water until it is almost shoulder deep, Stoney slides off and begins washing the great horse in the cold water.

When Stoney has finished washing his horse, he swims to the edge of the pool and begins walking with Roamer at his side up the little knoll to the log house. Roamer stops twice to shake the water off like a big dog. At the log house, Stoney stops to rub his horse's head and talks quietly to him while he dries him off with a gunnysack Black Eagle has left for him. Then Roamer turns and trots back to his pasture where he resumes his grazing.

Stoney walks up the stairs to the porch, and picking up the towel, begins drying himself off. He's almost finished when the screen door opens and Black Eagle steps out carrying a tray loaded with dishes.

"Breakfast is served."

"It looks great, and just in time, I'm starved."

"Then sit down and dive in while I get the biscuits and honey."

When Black Eagle returns with the biscuits and honey, he asks, while setting the dishes on the table, "Have you thought anymore about what you're going to do after graduation?"

"I talked a little about it to Mom and Dad; I told them I might go down the road doing a little bull riding."

"Well you've always liked to do that, and you're pretty good at i."

"That's not why I want to do it… I thought it would give me a chance to travel almost anywhere in the country without attracting too much attention."

"That's what I meant when I told you to be invisible when you went among the people, kind of like hiding the tree in the forest."

"Yeah, I kind of thought that was what you had in mind."

"Pass the honey." Then, while spreading honey on his biscuit, "If you decide to do this, when are you planning on leaving?"

"We're having finals for the next three weeks and after that, I want to help move one of the herds up from the southern pasture."

Nodding his head in understanding, then asks, "When do you have to go home?"

"I promised Dad I'd be there when they got back from their hunting trip. But I imagine it might take them a little time to get out of those mountains."

"Good, you can do the dishes."

Stoney's at the sink washing and Black Eagle is drying.

"You said I wasn't to tell anyone that I was White Buffalo, I suppose that even means Mom and Dad."

"For now, they will learn when the Great Spirit wants them to know and, as I told you, I don't think that time is too far off."

Looking at his grandfather. "I'm still scared'"

"I know you are, and that is a good sign."

7

Hunters Return

Stoney is setting the basket on the sink top when Peggy walks in.

"Oh, I wasn't expecting you so early. Is your grandfather alright?"

"He's fine Mom, and he said to thank you for the dinner. He also said you could cook almost as good as your mother."

"Well, coming from Dad, I'll take that as a complement because your grandmother was a great cook." Then while cutting a piece of pie "Now sit down there and have a piece of this apple pie. But be careful, it's right out of the oven and hot."

As Stoney is eating his pie, Peggy's at the sink rinsing the knife she used to cut the pie, when she glances out the window.

"Oh, here comes your Dad and Oh... Oh, my goodness!!"

Peggy rushes out to the motor court, followed closely by Stoney.

Peggy stands there in disbelief, with her hand covering her mouth... And can't really believe her eyes as she watches the muddy hunters get out of the jeep.

Stoney, on the other hand, can't seem to keep from smiling.

Dropping her hand away from her face, Peggy asks, "What in the world happened?"

While stamping his feet on the pavement, trying to knock some of the mud off his sixteen hundred dollar ostrich skin boots, William answers, "We almost got killed, that's what happened, and just look at my new boots."

David sounds off. "Your boots, look at my new shooting jacket, it's ruined."

Phil is standing there still holding his pants up and away from his stomach, almost crying. "I want to go home, even my shorts are full of mud." Then turning, Phil starts walking toward his Rolls Royce, still crying. "I just want to go home and change my shorts."

As Phil starts to open the car door, John calls out with his voice of authority. "Wait a minute Phil; you can't get in a car like that. Come over here."

Phil has no idea what John has in mind, but he slowly shuffles over to John who nods at Stoney. "Give me that hose and turn it on full blast."

Stoney hands the hose to his father and turns it on. John turns, "Now hold still Phil, while I wash the mud off."

As John uses the hose to wash the mud off Phil, William smiles and chuckles, "I'm next."

Peggy begins to laugh. "I'll get some towels and warm clothes for everyone."

As Peggy leaves, Phil reaches for the hose. "Let me have that hose for a minute." And taking the hose, begins squirting it down the front of his pants "Wheee, that's cold"

By this time everyone's laughing and John, getting almost as wet as Phil, says, "It's good to see we're still able to laugh at ourselves"

Peggy comes out of the house with her arms full of robes and towels.

Joining in the laughter, Peggy says, "I've got a warm robe for everyone. As soon as you wash the mud off, step over behind that car and get out of your wet clothes. Then after you dry yourself off, put a robe on, and go in the house to take a nice hot shower. When you're through I've got some warm clothes for everyone, and a cup of hot chocolate and a piece of hot apple pie."

David's grinning from ear to ear. "Maybe this isn't going to be such a bad day after all."

Phil is over behind his car, getting out of his wet clothes, and John is laughing as he squirts William off and thinking he can't remember when he's had more fun, says "Even though none of us fired a shot, this will be one hunting trip, none of us, will ever forget."

After everyone has had a hot shower and changed into warm clothes, they're all sitting around the kitchen table, having hot chocolate and hot apple pie with a scoop of vanilla ice cream, and laughing at each other while telling and retelling everything that happened to them.

Feeling a little guilty, Stoney is outside hosing the mud off the motor court, thinking that is the least he can do.

Peggy is serving John his dinner, that evening and tells him, "I'm sorry your hunting trip was ruined."

John can't help but laugh. "Ruined, it wasn't ruined. I never had so much fun in my life. If you could have seen Phil's face, when William stepped on his two-dollar compass...
Or William standing there in mud, up to his knees in his brand new sixteen hundred dollar ostrich skin boots. Or the expression on David's face when he was on his knees in all that mud, looking at his brand new forty-seven hundred dollar rifle covered in mud, and Phil just sitting down and sliding down that muddy bank on the seat of his pants.

I'll tell you that was the funniest thing I ever saw in my life. I was laughing so hard, I couldn't stand up." Shaking his head slowly while thinking about Phil sliding down that muddy bank, then continuing, "I'm just glad they could finally see the humor in it". Chuckling, "I have to tell you, I was really beginning to think we were all getting a little too big for our britches. We were all taking ourselves too serious, and today's experience took us all down a notch or two. Which I'm afraid we all need every once in awhile as a reminder of our humility."

Looking a little sheepish, Stoney says, "I'm just glad no one got hurt."

"Hurt, the only thing that got hurt was their pride, and by Monday morning their pride will be healed and they'll be telling everyone about their exciting brush with near death." Then, looking at Stoney, "And while I was sitting under that pine tree and was finally able to stop laughing, I had a chance to look around. Looking up at those big beautiful, rugged mountains, with the rain running down my face and with the lightning lighting the whole mountain up like day, I knew you were right. Those mountains are too magnificent to allow anyone to destroy." Nodding his head, "I really want to get a better look at them in the daylight, so I've decided to go back up there to look for Phil's two dollar compass." Laughing, "I want to put it in my new trophy case and I thought I might look around while I'm up there."

"I've seen those mountains Dad and, believe me, they're beyond magnificent."

"Well in that case, do you suppose we could maybe spend a couple of days up there camping?"

'That's a great idea Dad, and we couldn't find a better place to camp. Let's do it real soon."

Looking at her two men with pride, Peggy asks Stoney.

"Do you still plan on traveling after graduation? "

"Yes, but I want to help with moving the cattle from the south pasture first."

John nods his head. "All right then, let's go down and look at some motor homes."

Shaking his head, "Thanks dad, but I don't want a motor home. If you don't mind, I'd like to take one of the old ranch pickups and horse trailer."

"Of course, we've got several new ones, just take your pick. But what's wrong with your truck? It's better than any of the ranch trucks."

"That's exactly what's wrong with it Dad. I don't want to go down the road as Stoney Wood of Wood Oil. I want to get out there and get to know people on their terms, to see how they live and I feel I can do that best by becoming one of them." Then looking at his mother and father. "I hope you understand."

Peggy is the first to speak. "Of course we do, but those are old trucks, and old trucks seem to have a habit of breaking down, at least ours always did."

Smiling at what his mother said, "I thought of that, and I thought I'd pick out a fairly decent one and have a new engine and transmission put in it. Then it should be fairly dependable, and I thought I'd even have a CB installed."

"And be sure you get new brakes and new tires on it."

John adds. "A CB is great for checking road conditions with the truckers, but don't forget to take your satellite phone along. And, you better have a new floor put in the horse trailer and be sure to have the electric brakes checked. Talk to Jim, he's our best mechanic, let him help you pick out a good truck and horse trailer."

Peggy shows her worry as mothers always seem to do, "But where are you going to sleep."

Putting his hand on his mother's hand. "I'll take my bedroll." Then "Don't worry Mom, I'll be all right, and thanks... Thanks to both of you for understanding. Now, if you'll excuse me, I think I better start hitting those books."

John and Peggy watch him leave, and after he's left the room John puts his hand on Peggy's. "Don't worry honey he's going to be all right, and I'll have a talk with Jim myself to be sure he goes over both the truck and trailer with a fine tooth comb. He'll be all right."

Peggy smiles at him and nods her head. "I know he will, it's just that I've always worried about him... As I've worried about both of you."

Stoney is sitting at his desk while taking notes from open books, then turning and typing on his computer. The clock on his night stand reads 2:15... A few pictures of Native Americans, a dream catcher, a victory ring, and a battle shield decorate the walls. Along with several pictures of Stoney, one as a child on a pony, another a little older, riding bulls, and yet another wearing his third degree black belt. Along with several pictures of his boyhood heroes'.

Several weeks later at Black Eagle Valley, Black Eagle and Stoney are standing just outside the arena watching the dancers.

"Now that you've finished finals, when are you leaving?"

"Not for at least another three weeks. We're starting to gather cattle in the south pasture tomorrow morning."

"Are you taking Roamer?"

"Are you kidding, he enjoys gathering cattle as much as or even more than, I do."

Stoney and Roamer spend the next several weeks with the other hands. Up before dawn and out on either side of the gathered herd that is slowly moving north. Methodically, scouring every creek bed, gully, and canyon in the southern pastures for strays and newborn calves, then herding them to the main herd where the calves are branded inoculated and castrated before rejoining their mothers and the main herd.

Late evening would find almost everyone gathered around the mechanized chuck wagon, being, served tin plates piled high with sizzling hot tasty steaks, mashed potatoes with gravy, baked beans, biscuits and gravy and lots of hot apple pie and hot coffee.

Then everyone gatherers around one of the many campfires with their dinner plates, laughing and expanding on past escapades.

While the nighthawks, waiting to be relieved for their dinner ride slowly around the gathered herd talking quietly or singing softly to keep the herd calm.

When the day is done and Roamer has been brushed and given a good serving of oats. Stoney stretches out in his bedroll. This time spent gazing at the stars is what Stoney feels is the best part of the day. Where he feels closest to his mother earth, and nearest to his Creator.

When Stoney is back at the ranch, after helping move the herd to one of the northern pastures, he spends almost half a day going over the old Chevy pickup truck and horse trailer with Jim. Unknown to Stoney, his father also spends a half day with Jim doing the same thing.

When Stoney arrives at Black Eagle Valley that evening, he finds his grandfather waiting for him in his tepee, sitting by the fire holding his sacred pipe. Taking his boots off and slipping on his moccasins, he sits across from his grandfather.

Who asks, "When are you leaving?"

"Saturday morning."

"Do you know where you're going?"

"No, I just feel I have to go, and I know he will show me the way"

Black Eagle nods his head, as if understanding, "Will I be seeing you before you leave?"

"Of course, I'll be over Saturday morning to pick Roamer up. But even if I wasn't, you know I could never leave without seeing you."

Black Eagle nods and unfastening a small leather bag from his belt, he opens it, after removing a small white object, hands it to Stoney. "This is a White Buffalo carved from the bones of a white buffalo. It was meant to be yours, and I have carried it for you since before you were born.

Wear it in your medicine bag. It will warn you and protect you from your enemies."

Turning it between his fingers, Stoney examines the intricately carved and polished figure.

"Thank you Grandfather, it's beautiful." Loosening his medicine bag, he does as instructed, and places it in his medicine bag.

Black Eagle turns and picks up a package wrapped in heavy brown wrapping paper and tied with a heavy white cord. Handing the package to Stoney, "This sacred ceremonial regalia was made for White Buffalo… Wear it with honor and pride."

"Thank you Grandfather. As you say, I will wear it with honor and pride." Pausing, then "And I would have you know, you have always been my strength and I'm going to miss you and your wisdom."

"You have two grandfathers now. The Great Spirit will be with you always, and I shall always be with you in your heart and in your campfires."

"As you have always been in my heart."

"As you have always been in mine." Setting his sacred pipe aside. "Now let us watch the prayer dancers, for they are dancing a prayer to the great Spirit for the success and safe return of one of our warriors."

Surprised, Stoney asks, "Do they know?"

Black Eagle shakes his head, "About White Buffalo, no. They only know one of our warriors has something important to do that is why we will not go to the sweat lodge to purify your inner being until after the dancers have left."

"I don't feel like a warrior."

"But you are a warrior, you are his warrior, and you will carry the warrior spirit of all our warriors with you."

8

The Quest

Worrying about his horse standing for so many hours in the trailer, Stoney turns off the busy interchange onto one of the secondary highways where he begins looking for a place where he can get off the highway to let Roamer stretch his legs. Or maybe, if he's lucky, even find a place to spread his bedroll.

However, after driving the old two-toned brown Chevrolet pickup truck with its matching two-horse trailer, through several small farming and ranching communities all he sees, are well-fenced farms with big immaculately maintained houses well off the highway. Not quite the type of place you would expect to be hospitable toward a down at the heels rodeo cowboy.

He's about to give up hope of finding a rest stop anytime soon when coming around a bend he sees on the right a little farm house with a sagging three-strand barbwire fence. And to his surprise, a farmer in bib overalls plowing his field with, of all things in this day and age, a mule.

Stoney pulls the truck over beside the road, gets out and walks over to the farmer, who has stopped his plowing to watch him approach

Looking the farmer over, it doesn't take Stoney long to decide this is a good man. Late forties, tall, coal black hair, already gray at the temples, callused hands, wearing a worn long sleeved sweat stained shirt under his bib overalls and worn brogans. Looking at the plowed field, Stoney notes their furrows are as straight as a string.

Stoney greets him. "Afternoon, been goin down the road since early morning, and I'm lookin for a place to let my horse out to stretch his legs and maybe a place to throw my bedroll for the night."

The farmer looks him over and then nods his head. "Down by the cottonwoods, a little stream down thar, not much, but it'll do you."

"Thanks much, I'm obliged."

The farmer nods his head again. "No bother." Then immediately resumes his plowing.

Driving the truck across the old cattle guard and down to the cottonwoods, he unloads Roamer. After he rolls, Stoney rubs him down and gives him some oats and a couple of flakes of hay.

Then building a little campfire and getting a little water from the stream to put a pot of coffee on, he begins preparing his dinner. Wrapping a couple of potatoes and an ear of corn in aluminum foil, he buries them in the hot coals. Then taking a pork steak out of its wrapping, impales it on a long thin green cottonwood branch. Hanging the steak over the fire to roast, Stoney leans back on his bedroll, enjoying the mouth-watering aroma of his dinner cooking on the open fire.

Listening to the water in the stream roll gently over the small stones in the creek bed and listening to the birds in the trees, while watching Roamer contentedly eat his hay, Stoney is thinking it can't get much better than this.

Then, thinking back to his greeting the farmer in the field and remembering the manner of speech he used in his greeting. A manner of speech he had never used in his life, and yet it had sounded and felt so natural he hadn't given it a second thought. Until now, suddenly realizing he had instinctively used that manner of speech, knowing he would not have been so readily accepted or trusted had he used his normal manner of speech.

Stoney's up before the crack of dawn, foregoing his normal running routine he has a quick breakfast, cleans his campsite, leaving no trace of his ever being there, and puts oats and hay in the trailer for Roamer. Then he is going down the road before the farmer has his mule hitched to his plow.

Towards afternoon the farms and ranches he's passing seem to be further and further apart.

About mid-afternoon, Stoney comes to a small river with an almost obscured dirt road overgrown with brush angling away from the highway. Slowing down and turning on the dirt road, Stoney slowly drives along the river until he finds a clearing that is well off the highway next to the river with some tall trees overhanging the river.

Making a wide turn, he parks the truck and trailer under the trees, facing back down the road toward the highway. Unloading Roamer, he takes him to the river where he can have a good drink of cool water, then turns him loose so he can graze the lush grass along the riverbank.

Taking a small collapsible fishing rod from the back of the truck, he walks back to the river, where in just a few minutes, he has caught two nice perch for his dinner.

Later that evening, while sitting around his campfire gazing into its flames and listening to the crickets and the croaking of frogs, he notices a slight brightening of the flames and then an almost transparent image of an old café with some huge cottonwood trees in the background. Then suddenly the image begins to fade away.

Stoney sits there for a few minutes wondering if it was just his imagination and if not, what it could possibly mean.

When he crawls into his bedroll that night, he's no closer to finding an answer.

As he closes his eyes, he can still see the image of the old café in his minds eye. Just an old white washed building with a sign, Café on its roof.

He's up early the next morning and, after his usual 5 mile run takes a quick swim. After having a little warmed up fish and coffee for breakfast, he's back on the road.

Toward mid-day, he's watching the gas gage and thinking he should have filled up in that last little town he went through about forty miles back, when coming around a bend in the road he notices a little white building ahead. And if he's not mistaken, there are several old gasoline pumps out front and several old pickup trucks in front of the white building.

9

Lou's Cafe

Stopping his truck by two gas pumps with old type glass containers on top full of gasoline, Stoney's about to get out, when he notices the little white building has a sign on its roof, Café, and in little hand painted letters "Lou's". Another sign on the gas pump leaves no doubt as to its meaning, as it proclaims in big bold letters, PAY INSIDE FIRST.

Wearing old faded wranglers, a western shirt, an old pair of scuffed boots and an old beat up straw western hat, Stoney climbs out. Walking toward the café, Stoney notices the huge cottonwood trees and pauses for a moment, remembering the vision. He thinks to himself, "This is the café in the vision, but what does it mean."

Approaching the entry, he notices a flyer in the window by the front door advertising a rodeo in Riverton the following weekend. Then, along side the rodeo flyer, stuck to the window with a piece of sun-hardened scotch tape, another hand painted sign saying "Help Wanted." Pulling the help wanted sign off the dirty window; Stoney enters the café and steps over to the cash register. He stands there a few minutes, waiting for a waitress wearing a light green uniform to finish writing something in her order book. Cindy very attractive, early twenties, sparkling green eyes, dark brown hair with just a tinge of red, puts her order book in her apron pocket and the pen behind her ear, then looking up at Stoney, steps over to the register and without expression asks. "Yeah?"

"I'd like twenty dollars of unleaded, and can you tell me where Riverton is?"

"About 10, maybe 12 miles straight down the road," Pausing while, slowly shaking her head, "You thinking about the rodeo?"

"I thought I might give it a try". Setting the help wanted sign on the counter, "What about this help wanted sign? Can you tell me what kind of help you need?"

"Busing tables, washing dishes, cleaning up... As if this dump was ever clean. Why, you interested?"

"I might be but I'll probably be leaving after the rodeo."

"That's longer than most help stays around here. But you must be crazy to even think about working in this dump."

"You're working here."

"Yeah, but I've got a six year old kid to take care of. But if you're serious, I'll tell Lou you want to talk to him, he's the boss."

Nodding, "I'd appreciate it."

Looking at him, as if to see if he's really serious, then shrugging her shoulders, Cindy turns and walks over and says something to the cook. The cook glances at Stoney, then says something to Cindy, who turns and returns to where Stoney's standing,

"He'll be right here." Then smiling, "As soon as he finishes burning whatever he's cooking."

Smiling, Stoney asks. "Do you live around here?"

"Nobody lives around here, we just exist.... But yeah I rent one of those leaky cabins out back from Lou, which he charges too much for."

"If it leaks, why doesn't he fix the roof?"

"He say's it only leaks when it rains, and he never wants to get up there when it's raining because he'd get wet."

"You're kidding."

"I only wish I was."

Lou comes out of the kitchen. He is in his late forties and his baldhead is glistening with perspiration, wearing a white soiled tee shirt, soiled white pants, and a soiled white apron He's wiping, his greasy hands on the seat of his soiled pants, and he doesn't look like he's shaved in a week.

Nodding his head in Cindy's direction, "She says you want the job. Ever wash dishes?"

"Only my own."

Cindy begins to smile, while Lou asks, "Ever bus tables?"

"No."

"Well it ain't hard to learn... You're hired, minimum wage an all you can eat, as long as you don't eat too much."

'Thanks, but I have to tell you I'll probably only be here for about a week."

Repeating what Cindy had said. "That's longer than most of them last."

"I saw a grove of cottonwoods out back, do you mind if I camp down there?"

"You don't want to rent one of my cabins?"

"I think I'd rather camp out. Besides, I've got my horse with me and I'd like to let him graze if it's all right with you."

"It's ain't fenced for horses."

"That's alright he won't wander off."

"Whatever, grass is cheap. There's a stream down there, just don't make no messes. I can't stand no messes."

Trying to suppress his smile, "I can see that."

Lou nods in Cindy's direction, "She'll tell you what to do, just be ready for the evening rush."

Muttering, as he walks back to the kitchen. "A horse."

Cindy's smiling as she watches him go. "I wish I'd thought of that."

"What's that?"

"Camping out... Oh... That rush he's talking about is probably thirty people... If we're lucky."

Stoney goes out front and fills his truck with gas, then drives down to the cottonwoods where he unloads Roamer and throws some hay out for him, then walks back to the café where he finds Cindy waiting for him by the back door.

"I saw you unload your horse, aren't you afraid he'll wander off?"

"No, he won't go anywhere."

"Come on, I'll show you where the aprons are, and contrary to popular belief we really do have some clean aprons.

As he's tying his apron, he has to smile when Cindy tells him. 'And you probably won't need that hat in here; you can leave it on top of your locker. But don't believe that either, it doesn't lock" Cindy says, then, "Follow me and I'll give you the grand tour." Pointing toward a large stainless steel sink, cluttered with dirty dishes "This is where you'll be doing your pearl diving." Pausing, then explaining, "That means where you wash the dishes."

Seeing some customers are leaving, she picks up a large deep plastic tub and a damp towel.

"C'mon, I'll teach you the fine art of bussing a table."
Stoney follows her into the dinning area, where she sets the tub on the table, then gathering the dishes up, dumps them into the tub and as she wipes the table with the damp towel, she picks up the tip.

"Real big spenders… Four people and all they could afford was half a buck. And they'll probably take it as a tax deduction under the category, charitable contributions. Well at least I'll never have to worry about getting rich working in this dump."

Using the towel she finishes wiping the table, pushing the litter in the tub. Then she arranges the salt and peppershakers in the center of the table with the sugar bowl and napkin dispenser.

"Then you take the tub to your sink, separate the dishes from the garbage, stacking the dishes up until you have a good stack. After you wash them, you stack the clean dishes back in the kitchen so Lou can mess them up again. And like Lou says, it ain't hard to learn."

As Cindy starts to pick the tub up, Stoney takes it out of her hands and, as he's carrying it to the kitchen, asks "Is that all there is to it?"

"That's only the beginning, bussing the counter is about the same, even easier. But Lou doesn't want us to stand around, so when we don't have anything else to do, we fill the salt and pepper shakers and the catsup bottles and never let Lou see you fill a catsup bottle, without putting a little water in it first?"

"Why should I put water in a catsup bottle?"

"Because it's cheaper than catsup."

"I don't think I could do that, that's cheating the customers."

Surprised. "I don't think Lou ever bothered to consider that. But you can leave the catsup bottles to me, I'll take care of them. Then when we really don't have anything to do, we sweep and mop the floors, but as you can see that doesn't happen too often."

Then looking at her watch. "Oh, Sally should be here any minute so I better get ready to leave, I have to be in Riverton in a half hour."

"Who's Sally?"

"She's the other waitress. It's really her day off, but she's coming in because I have to leave." And nodding toward the window, "Here she comes now."

Glancing out the window, Stoney sees a tall red-haired woman in her mid thirties, wearing a waitress uniform, just getting out of an old blue pickup.

Sally enters and Cindy makes the introductions. Then, going behind the counter removes her apron, slips into a sweater, picks up her purse and heads toward the door saying, "I better run… I'll see you guys in the morning."

Sally calls out. "Give my love to Tim."

Cindy waves as she leaves

Stoney asks. "Is Tim her husband?"

"No, her son, he's at Riverton Community Hospital."

One of the customers calls out. "Can we have a check over here?"

Sally answers. "I'll be right with you."

Putting on her apron, Sally goes to the table and gives the customer his check. The customer goes to the register and Sally goes there to ring it up.

Stoney picks up a tub and a damp towel and starts bussing the table, leaving the seventy-five cent tip on the table. More customers come in. Sally seats them and gives them a menu and as she passes Stoney. ""Will you get them some water while I check on the other customers?"

Stoney gets a tray and four glasses of water and takes it to the new customers.

Then going to where Sally is picking up an order. "Would you like me to check all the tables to see if they all have water?"

"That would be great." Then, looking at Stoney, Sally asks, "Have you ever bussed before?"

"No. I've just seen it done and I really don't know what I'm doing, so if you need anything, just ask."

"Don't worry about it, it never gets too busy in here, because the food's too lousy." Seeing more people walk in, "Some more customers just came in, will you take them some water and a menu, and tell them I'll be right there?"

A few more customers arrive during the dinner hours. With customers coming in and customers leaving, Stoney finds he has to hurry, but manages to clean the tables as soon as they leave, and is right there with water and a menu when new customers arrive, and even finds time to wash a load of dishes.

When business seems to have quieted down, Stoney is clearing off a table when Sally walks over. "Have you had dinner yet?"

"Not yet."

"Then get rid of those dishes and we'll have something to eat."

Sitting next to Sally at the end of the counter, Stoney picks up a menu and Sally nudges him with her elbow. "Take my advice and don't order anything that comes off Lou's grill... Try some baked chicken, that's safe and its usually pretty good."

Smiling, "You talked me into it, but is Lou's cooking really as bad as I've been hearing?"

Chuckling, Cindy says his advertising," home style cooking," is next to blasphemous. Then when a customer finds a cockroach in their scrambled eggs and I show the scrambled eggs to Lou so he won't think the customer was just trying to cheat him, and he goes through the eggs with a spoon to see if he can find another roach before admitting there is anything wrong with the eggs... I'd say that's pretty bad..."

"I think I may have just lost my appetite."

Laughing,"Come on, you should be all right with either the baked chicken or the baked ham."

"All right, I'll have the baked chicken." Then, while their waiting for their dinner Stoney asks, "Why's Cindy's son in the hospital?"

Hesitantly, "He's got leukemia."

"Oh, no... How old is he?"

"Six... And he's really a great kid; even Lou has a soft spot in his heart for him. But they've tried chemotherapy, and it didn't help, now they want to try a bone marrow transplant... If they can find a match."

"How long has he been in the hospital?"

"He's not in the hospital all the time. Cindy doesn't have any insurance, so the hospital only keeps him a few days at a time, when they run their tests."

"Is he getting good treatment under those circumstances?"

"Surprisingly yes, the hospital seems to be doing everything they can and have never sent Cindy a bill."

"Where's her husband?"

"He was killed almost three years ago, bull riding."

"Three years ago… What was his name?"

"He was a Navajo, Jim Light Horse Morris."

"Oh, no… I knew him; he was a second year geology student when I was in my first year at Oklahoma."

"It's a small world."

"I didn't know him very well, I'd run into him on campus once in awhile and I'd see him at the rodeos. I remember when it happened. A bull turned on him before he could get out of the arena. I wasn't there, but when something like that happens all the riders on the circuit hear about it."

"Did you graduate from Oklahoma?"

"Yeah."

"If you graduated from Oklahoma, what the heck are you doing bussing tables at a dump like Lou's?"

Smiling, "You think I should be bussing tables in a higher class establishment?"

Laughing, "No, you know what I mean, why are you bussing at all?"

Turning to look her in the eyes, "Would you believe me if I told you, I just wanted to go down the road and I couldn't think of a better way to do it?"

"Yeah, I'd believe that. I think we all get feeling like that once in awhile, but the rest of us just don't have the nerve to get up and do it."

10

Wishing on a Star

Later that evening, while sitting around his campfire
having a cup of coffee,
Stoney is thinking about what Sally told him about Cindy and
her son, when Roamer goes into his alert mode, raising his
head with ears cocked forward peering into the darkness
telling him someone is approaching the camp. Then a few
minutes later.

"Hello... Anyone home?"

Stoney stands as Cindy walks into camp, wearing a faded
pair of jeans, loafers, a white tee shirt and a light sweater.

"I think I heard somewhere that you were supposed to call
out before you entered anyone's camp."

Smiling, "Well it's probably a pretty good idea, but I think
you may have been watching too much television. But since
you're here, haul up a log and make yourself at home while I
pour a cup of coffee for you."

Cindy sits by the fire, leaning back against a large log,
while holding her hands out toward the warmth of the fire.
Stoney pours the coffee and handing it to her. "Would you like
some cream or sugar?"

"No thanks, black is fine. I hope you don't mind my
barging in on you this way, but I couldn't sleep and when I

saw your fire, I thought I'd pay a little visit to my new neighbor."

"I'm glad you did… How's Tim?"

Cindy looks surprised and Stoney explains. "Sally told me."

A little smile of understanding fleets across her face. "About the same, they won't have the results of the latest series of tests for several days. In the meantime all I can do is hope."

"What's the prognosis?"

"Not very good, and I don't mind admitting I'm getting scared."

"Of course you're scared, but don't give up hope."

"I don't know… Hope comes and goes in degrees, and now we're running out of options. If they don't find a bone marrow match soon, I don't know what we'll do. And their finding a match is even more difficult because Tim's father was Native American, making the possibility of finding a match extremely slim."

"I'm Native American and while I'm not Navajo, I'll go in for a test tomorrow."

'Thank you. I thought you were. What tribe?

"Cherokee."

"You knew Jim was Navajo?"

"Yes, I knew Jim slightly, both at school and rodeos."

Slowly shaking her head. "When you told me you were going to the rodeo in Riverton, my stomach tied up in knots. But, you're not going to ride any bulls are you?"

"Probably."

Sounding angry, "What's the matter with you guys, are you all nuts? Those are wild animals, two thousand pounds of wild animal, and you nuts want to see if you can ride them. You're all crazy."

"I know, and don't ask me to explain it, I took several pre-psychology courses in school and I still can't explain it. I think it's something you really have to experience to understand.

When you get on that bull's back and they throw the gate open the adrenaline starts rushing through your body and when your bull takes that first jump out of the chute, it's the highest high in the world. It's just you and that bull for the next eight seconds, with both of you wanting to find out who's best."

"It's not the money?"

Laughing, "It's definitely not the money, most rodeos don't pay enough to cover the cost of your bandages."

"Yeah, you're all nuts... But I don't want to talk about it anymore."

"What do you want to talk about?"

"Well, we can start with your telling me what you do out here without a television?"

Laughing and motioning toward the sky. "I've got the biggest television in the world right up there and I never have to change a channel, it changes constantly all by itself. Then pointing into the night sky, while Cindy leans back against the log to look where he's pointing.

"There's the big dipper, there's Orion's belt and look there, a shooting star, that's always a good sign."

"When I was a little girl, I used to wish on the stars. Like... Star light, star bright the first star I see tonight, I wish I may, I wish I might, have this wish I wish tonight... Crazy eh?"

"That would have been the evening star you were wishing on, and wishing on stars isn't crazy at all because sometimes wishes have strange ways of coming true. And if you could wish on a star tonight, what would you wish for?"

With the hint of tears glistening in her eyes, Cindy answers, "I'd only have one wish, and that would be for my son."

"Jim was Navajo; did you go to the tribe for help?"

"I didn't know I could, besides Timmy is only half Navajo, what many people call a half breed. And nobody seems to care about one little kid."

"Your wrong Cindy, with just one drop of blood, he would still be Indian, and a tribe is like a large extended family that cares very much for every child. They believe every child is important. In fact, children are almost sacred to Native Americans."

"But don't you think they're too busy with their gambling casinos?"

"I don't know where you got your information, but it's wrong. The Navajo Nation has refused to allow gambling casinos on Indian property, because they feel gambling is immoral.

True there are factions within the tribe who support the idea of allowing casinos but the tribe has voted them down time and time again." Then Stoney asks, "Have you ever visited the Navajo reservation?"

"No, I didn't even know we could visit the reservation."

"They welcome all visitors and I'm really surprised you haven't done so, especially living so close, and it's so beautiful."

"I heard the reservation in Arizona was the prettiest."

Chuckling, "It's all one reservation, it's a little over twenty-five thousand square miles, extending into four States New Mexico, Arizona, Utah and Colorado and it's all beautiful, in its own way. Your husband was Navajo and I know, even from the few times I spoke with him, he was extremely proud of his heritage, as all Navajos should be."

"Yes, I know, he was very proud of his heritage, and I really would like to see the reservation." Pausing a moment, then asking, is it true Navajos still live in Hogan's?"

"First, I should probably explain, the word Hogan in Navajo means home. But I know what you mean, a house built of logs and brush and covered with mud. What is called a traditional Hogan. And, yes many Navajos still live in traditional Hogan's, mainly because they choose to live in the traditional way, the way their ancestors lived.

But you will also find many Hogan's built of wood, stone, brick and stucco. You will also find apartments, condominiums and high rise buildings.

The Navajo are truly a remarkable people. The Navajo are governed by 80 council members, men and women, all elected by their peers, who meet with their chairman, vice-chairman and speaker four times a year to discuss tribal business, and that's exactly what it is, a discussion without partisan politics. Our politicians in Washington should really take a few lessons from them, you should be proud your son is Navajo."

"I really am and Tim's asked me a thousand questions about his Indian heritage, I'm ashamed I've never taken the time to take him to the reservation."

"What about Jim's family?"

"Jim never talked much about his family; only that he had a disagreement with his mother and left home.
He told me I shouldn't worry about it because he was working on the problem." Looking at her watch. "It's getting late, I better be going."

"I'll walk you home."

"You must be some kind of Boy Scout; I haven't had anyone walk me home in years." And as they are walking toward Cindy's cabin. "If you're serious about going to the hospital for a bone marrow test, we can go together tomorrow evening after work and you can meet Timmy."

"I'd like that very much."

As they approach the cabins, Stoney takes Cindy's hand to help her up a small embankment. Stumbling, Cindy finds herself in Stoney's arms. Looking into her eyes, he sees the reflection of the stars. Putting her arms around Stoney, Cindy holds him tight and with their hands exploring each other they kiss… Cindy slowly relaxes her arms and steps back a step and looking into his eyes. "I think I better go in."

Nodding, "Goodnight Cindy, I'll see you in the morning."

Stoney watches as she steps inside, and slowly closes the door. Then, with a lot to think about, he slowly walks back to his camp, where he places a few small logs on his campfire and sits while gazing into its flames, asking the Great Spirit to show him a sign.

Stoney is cleaning the windows when Cindy arrives for work. "What in the world are you doing? Those windows haven't been cleaned since I've been here, and probably years before that."

Wiping the squeegee with a towel, he answers, "I just thought I'd like to see what they looked like if they were clean."

Shaking her head in amazement, then glancing at the wall clock, Cindy says, "We've still got thirty minutes before we open so if you put the bucket away and have a seat, I'll get a cup of coffee for you."

"Could I have a glass of juice instead?"

As she sets a glass of orange juice on the counter, "I saw you earlier this morning while you were running, do you run every morning?"

"I try to."

Cindy smiles, "Don't you get a little cold running around like that?"

A little embarrassed, Stoney says, "Maybe I better start wearing some sweats."

"Hey, don't do that on my account, I wasn't complaining" Then laughing "Besides, it helps get my blood circulating, without my having to work up a sweat."

Lou comes in the back door, and is tying a grease-soiled apron on as he walks into the kitchen.

Then hollering, "What happened to the floor?"

Looking puzzled, Cindy hurries to the kitchen, and then bursts out laughing. "That's the way it's supposed to look, clean."

Shaking his head, "You should tell me when you do these things."

"You can't blame this on me. It must have been Stoney, but don't worry, I'll tell him not to do it again, that you like the floor dirty."

Shaking his head. "No, clean is all right."

Then looking at Lou's dirty apron and shaking her head, "Why don't you at least put on a clean apron, to go with your clean floor?"

Still looking at the clean floor, "Maybe I will... But the customers never come back here.

"You should be thankful they don't, and may god forbid the health department from ever coming back here."

Then she returns, wearing a smile, to where Stoney is finishing his orange juice. "You better be careful, I don't think his heart will take too much of that." Looking at the clock on the wall. "Well I guess we better get this dump open.

Two truck drivers are waiting to get in as Cindy unlocks the front door. Showing them to a table, she gives them a menu and tells them she will be right back for their order. Returning from their table, she passes Stoney who is busy cleaning behind the counter, shaking her head in amazement. "You keep that up and you'll ruin our reputation."

Several more customers enter and, seeing Cindy is busy picking up the trucker's order, Stoney stops cleaning to take them some water and a menu. He tells them the waitress will be right with them and then returns to his cleaning.

Cindy takes the truckers their order, then stepping over to the new customers begins taking their order, when the front door opens and two young cowboys walk in and seat themselves at an adjoining table. Cindy turns and handing them each a menu. "I'll be right back to take your order and bring you some water."

As she passes Stoney, she quietly says. "That Cliff Walker is always trouble."

Stoney looks at the two cowboys and watches as Cindy places her latest order, and is just starting back when Lou rings the bell, as he places an order ready for pickup on the pass through.

Turning back Cindy picks up the order and carries it to one of the tables. Then goes to the cowboys table to take their order.

The truck drivers motion for their check. Giving them their check, Cindy hurries to the register to accept their payment and ring it up.

As Cindy starts to the kitchen to place the order from the cowboys table, Cliff Walker, young, broad shoulders wearing jeans, boots and western hat, calls out, "Can't you hurry? We don't want to be here all day."

She hurries to place their order. "It'll just be a few minutes." As she places the order with Lou, "You better hurry this one Lou, this guy is always in a hurry and he's always trouble."

"Everyone's always in a hurry."

Lou throws another order on the pass through and rings the pickup bell.

Cindy picks up the order and hurries to one of the tables. She places the dishes in front of the customers and is freshening their coffee. When Cliff calls out, "Did you tell him to hurry with that order?"

Glaring at him, "I always tell him to hurry your order." Several customers snicker.

"Do you think we can have some coffee while we're waiting?" Cliff asks in a demanding voice.
Stoney picks up two cups and a pot of coffee, taking them to Cliff's table and pours the coffee.

Sarcastically, "Thanks Chief."

Ignoring the sarcasm, "No problem."

Cindy passes him as he's placing the coffee pot back on the hot plate. "Thanks."

Stoney only nods as Lou rings the bell and throws another order on the pass through. Picking up the order and a bottle of catsup, Cindy hurries to Cliff's table and while placing the dishes in front of the two cowboys. "Enjoy your breakfast."

Cliff looks Cindy up and down, while smiling, "We will." Cindy walks around the dinning area, stopping at several tables, asking the customers if there is anything else she can get for them, and filling a few coffee cups as she moves from table to table.

The group sitting next to Cliff's table goes to the cash register.

Setting the coffee pot down, Cindy goes to help them and Stoney starts bussing the table they have just vacated. When Cindy's finished at the register, she picks the coffee pot back up and starts circulating through the dinning area.

Suddenly added to the usual hum of normal conversation of the dinning area is Cliff's booming voice calling out "Can't we get a little more coffee over here?"

"I'll be right there."

As Cindy steps up to the table and reaches over to fill Cliff's cup, he reaches around and pats her on the rear. Startled, Cindy steps back and as she does, without hesitation she pours the hot coffee in his lap.

Cliff screams, "Yeeeeeeeeeeeee" while jumping up from the table. "Ohhhhhh, my gawd! that's hot!," jumping around trying to pull his hot pants away from his privates. Then Cliff suddenly turns toward Cindy, "You burned me! You burned me! You burned me on purpose."

With a straight face, "I'm sorry sir, you startled me." starting to turn away, "I'll get a towel for you."

Cliff grabs Cindy by her arm, jerking her around, causing her to almost drop the empty coffee pot.

"You did that on purpose... I'll teach you. Drawing his arm back, he's about to hit Cindy with his closed fist when Stoney grabs his arm. "I don't think you really want to do that."

"Stay out of this Chief, this doesn't concern you."

"I'm afraid it does... Now why don't you just go home and change your pants?"

Looking down at his pants and around the dinning area where several customers have already started to get out of their chairs, then turning back to his table, "Come on Bob lets get the hell out of this dump." Then, turning back to Stoney, "You should have stayed out of this Chief, and I hope you don't think it's over, because it's not. Not by a long shot."

Stoney nods his head and watches them leave. Then from the kitchen, Lou calls out. "Hey, they didn't pay for their breakfast."

Laughing Stoney calls back. "Don't worry Lou, this is one breakfast I'll gladly pay for."

And another customer calls out "No you won't, I'm glad to see that jerk taken down a notch or two, so I'll pay just for the pleasure of seeing someone do it."

Stoney nods. "Thanks."

As Stoney starts to clean up the spilled coffee, Cindy comes over. "Let me help." As they're cleaning the floor, "Thanks Stoney, but you better be careful. He's got a bad reputation around here and he hangs out with a bunch of young cowboys who think they're tough and you can bet he'll be going to the rodeo...I just wish we had more truck drivers for customers, they are never any problem, but they usually just drive on by." Pausing she looks at the table, then laughs, "Darn it, he didn't even leave a tip."

11

Timmy Morris

The rest of the day is fairly un-eventful; except, surprisingly, Cindy receives several complements on Lou's cooking, and subsequently an increase in tips

Coming in, in the late afternoon to help with the dinner crowd, Sally has tears in her eyes from laughing so hard, when Cindy tells her about her run in with Cliff Walker.

"Darn I wish I had been here to see that. I'll bet that really took the starch out of his... Well, you know what I mean."

Stoney is driving and Cindy's in the passenger seat, as Stoney says, riding shotgun.

They're driving down a three lane highway for about twenty minutes when Stoney sees some lights ahead.

"Is that Riverton?"

"No, that's the entrance to the reservation."

"It looks like they keep some pretty late hours."

"Don't we all."

A few minutes later, Cindy points, "There, the light on the left, that's the hospital and the parking lot is just on the other side of the lights."

Stoney swings in the parking lot, and finds a parking space near the entrance.

As they are approaching the entry, Cindy thinks she should apologize, "I hope you don't mind, but I called the hospital earlier, and told them you would be coming in for a test."

"Of course I don't mind, in fact I'm glad you did. That probably gave them enough time to sharpen their needles."

When Cindy turns to look at him, Stoney says, "I'm only kidding."

"You better be, because I only told you because I didn't want you to wonder why they are all standing in the lab with their needles at the ready when you walk in."

"You make it sound like I was going to face a firing squad."

"Maybe I better shut up. You might get scared and leave."

"Not a chance, but just be sure they blindfold me first."

Cindy shows him to the lab. "I could say I'm going to leave because I hate the sight of blood. But I'm really anxious to see Timmy, so I'll just leave you in their good hands, when you're through, just walk down to the end of this corridor and turn left, Tim's room is the second on the right, room 112."

The lab tech takes Stoney's name address, phone number, health history and weight, and then draws a sample of blood for their tests.

As she's filling out more forms she asks. "If in the event you're not a match for this patient, would you be willing to be a donor for another patient in the future?"

"Of course, just call the number I gave you, someone there will always be able to reach me."

After signing the necessary forms, Stoney's on his way to meet Tim. Turning into room 112, he's greeted by Cindy's radiant smile as she gets up from sitting on the edge of Tim's bed. "Stoney, I'd like you to meet my son Tim. Tim this is my friend Stoney."

Holding his hand out, "Hi Tim, I'm sure glad to meet you. Your mom's been telling me a lot about you."

And smiling, "Come to think about it, she never seems to stop talking about you."

Shaking Stoney's big hand, "I'm glad to meet you too, and she's told me a lot about you too. Is it true you're going to be in the rodeo?"

"Oh, she told you that eh? Well I guess that's true enough."

"Can I come to watch you?"

"Of course, I'd love to have you there… That is if it's all right with your Mom."

"I told him he should ask you, but are you sure it's all right?"

"Of course I'd love to have you both there to root for me… You would be rooting for me wouldn't you?"

Backhanding him lightly on the shoulder, "And who else do you think I'd be rooting for?"

"Well I don't know, but I'm sure you'll probably know one or two of the other participants."

Getting a little irritated at his obvious reference to Cliff. "You keep that up and I will be rooting for someone else, the bull."

Tim's eyes are as big as saucers. "Are you really going to ride a bull?"

"Just a little one."

Cindy shakes her head. "Yeah, they don't make any little bulls."

"And Mom says you have a horse… Can I ride him?"

Laughing, "Boy, Mom has been busy." Then, looking at Tim, asks, "Have you ever ridden a horse?"

A little hesitantly, Tim answers, "Well… No, but I've ridden a pony."

"Well that counts, so I guess you aren't a greenhorn… When do the doctors say you can get out of here?"

"Tomorrow," Then, looking at his mother. "I think."

"That's what the doctor told me so I'll pick you up tomorrow afternoon as soon as I can get away from work."

"Then tomorrow it is, is that soon enough?"

Excitedly,"You bet.. Ohhh. My gosh, I can't wait"… Then, "What's his name? What color is he?"

Seeing the excitement in Timmy's eyes, Stoney smiles. "His name is Roamer and he's a black and white paint stallion… And he'll be waiting for you to get home tomorrow."

"Roamer… That's a funny name, what's it mean?"

"Roamer means to travel or wander from place to place, so I guess he's kind of like me, a wanderer."

"Oh boy, I can hardly wait."

Cindy holds his hand. "But you have to promise to get some rest tonight and remember what the doctor said about not getting too excited."

"I will Mom, I promise."

"Did the doctor say anything about ice cream?"

"No, I don't think so."

"Good, because I saw an ice cream machine in the hall, so what do you think about my getting us all some ice cream?"

"Can I have chocolate?"

"And, what about you Mom?"

Laughing, "I'll have chocolate too."

It wasn't the best ice cream in the world, but to Tim, Cindy and Stoney it seemed like it was.

Cindy is very quiet on the way home at least for the first ten minutes. Then, "Thanks."

"For what?"

"For being so nice to Tim… I could tell he really likes you."

"You don't need to thank me, he's a good kid and I really like him too."

Then after another ten minutes of silence. "Is it true what you said?"

"What I said, about what?"

"About being a wanderer?"

Thinking about it for a moment, "Yeah, I guess that would be as good a description of me as any."

"But why, did you come from a broken home?"

"No, I come from a well adjusted home and my parents are still very much in love. It's just that there are some things I feel I must do, things I feel I have to do, at least for the present."

'That sounds very mysterious."

"Yes, I suppose it does."

Everything is dark by the time they get back to the closed café, the only light being a small 40 watt bulb lighting the entry to Cindy's little cabin.

"I think I should probably apologize for not being more talkative on the way home, and I hope you don't think it's the company... It's just that I seem to go into a state of depression every time I have to leave him in the hospital. I always imagine what he's thinking and going through every time he sees his mother go home, leaving him there."

"That's understandable and I know what you must be going through. But remember what I said... Don't give up, remember the stars."

Getting out of the truck, "I won't, and thanks again for helping to make Tim so happy. Goodnight.

"Goodnight Cindy, I'll see you in the morning."

Driving down to the cottonwoods and parking the truck, he puts some kindling on to start the fire, and throws Roamer a little more hay. Then sitting before the fire he gazes into its flames, when the little White Buffalo in his medicine bag begins to pulsate.

The camp fire has burned down to red hot coals glowing in the night. Stoney's bedroll is spread out near the fire and Roamer is calmly grazing just outside the camp area, when four figures silently creep through the darkness and approach the camp, stepping very quietly they step up to the sleeping form. Suddenly Cliff Walker kicks at the sleeping form. "I told you this wasn't over..." Surprised, " Waaa... He's not here."

"Stepping out of the darkness, wearing deer skin breeches, moccasins, and a colored headband, Stoney asks, "Where you looking for me?"

Turning to look at the figure standing behind them, "Damn, he really is an Indian... You should have stayed the hell out of my business Chief..." Then ordering, "Get him."

All four of them rush Stoney... But suddenly Roamer comes charging out of the darkness, rising up on his rear legs and tearing the night apart with his stallion scream, while pawing the air with his front hoofs knocking one of the intruders aside with his massive chest. While another is backing up so fast, he doesn't see the campfire, until he trips over a log, falling backwards and sitting down in the red hot coals. Letting out a scream he jumps up and runs to the stream and sits in the cold water.

Still advancing on Stoney, Cliff suddenly finds a moccasin covered foot alongside his head, knocking him to his knees. The other man, seeing what happened to his friends, suddenly turns and runs. Cliff, still on his knees, is slowly shaking his head.

Picking up a small pan, Stoney calmly walks to the stream, filling it with water. He then returns to Cliff and slowly pours the water over his head.

Then kneeling in front of him. "You'll be all right in a few minutes. But I hope you realize, you shouldn't drop in on people like this. It's really not very polite."

Cliff staggers to his feet, picks up his hat, and with water dripping from his lowered head slowly walks out of the camp, followed by his two friends

After straightening up around the camp and checking to be sure Roamer wasn't hurt, and putting a few more logs on the fire, Stoney stretches out in his bedroll thinking about Timmy and his leukemia while, wondering what he's expected to do for this terminally ill child.

12

The Truck Stop

Stoney is in the café cleaning when Cindy arrives.

"Don't you ever rest?" Laughing, "You're beginning to make the rest of us look bad. Come on over and have a seat while I get a glass of juice for you."

Stoney is sitting at the counter enjoying his orange juice, when Cindy inquires, "I know I shouldn't pry, but didn't I hear some hollering coming from your camp last night?"

Shaking his head, "I don't think I heard anything, but then I'm a heavy sleeper."

"Yeah, I'll bet."

Cindy is almost speechless as she watches Lou walk in freshly shaved, wearing clean white pants, a clean tee shirt, and watches in disbelief as he puts on a clean apron and a clean white chef's hat.

In a low voice, "My god, will you look at that, he actually looks like a real live chef."

Smiling, "And you have to admit, he has been cooking better lately."

"Yes he has, even the customers have been remarking about the good food and business has really been picking up."

Stoney gets up, walks around and puts his glass in the sink and smiling. "Come on, let's get this dump open."

Laughing, "Yeah that sounds familiar, and I better quit calling it a dump; it's starting to look like a real restaurant."

"Yeah, and we've even got real catsup in the catsup bottles."

As Cindy's about to open the door, "Will you look at that? There must be at least four trucks out there waiting for us to open."

"Truckers have a habit of talking to other truckers on the CB about good truck stops, and Lou may have to upgrade those gas pumps and maybe have another couple of diesel pumps installed."

Sally has to come in early to help with the steady flow of truckers who have been stopping for fuel and something to eat.

"My god, I really didn't believe you when you said we were busy. If this keeps up Lou's going to have to hire another waitress."

"And he's going to have to open earlier and stay open later. Can you imagine, there were four truckers waiting for us to open this morning? I think I should have a talk with Lou. If he'd just up grade those gas pumps like Stoney said and put another couple of diesel pumps in and clean up those cabins he'd have a real gold mine here."

"Yeah and those truckers aren't cheap, they leave some pretty good tips."

"You got that right, I just hope it's not a flash in the pan and they suddenly stop coming."

"Why would they do that? They all seem to enjoy the food, especially since Lou put out those new menus advertising his Trucker Specials."

"I know, but I still think it's kind of strange, how all of a sudden we've got every trucker on the road stopping here to eat, instead of just driving by like they've always done."

"Yeah, but don't knock it, lets just hope they keep coming."

"You're right and Lou's happy, he even told me to put Darlene on full time. I asked her to start this afternoon, because I have to pick Tim up at the hospital."

"That's great honey, how's the little guy doing?"

"About the same, but I'll know more after I talk to the Doctor."

"Well give him my love and remember, I'm praying for him."

"Thanks Sally."

Later that afternoon, as Stoney is going out to fill one of the trucks with diesel fuel, he passes Cindy as she's putting her sweater on. She remarks, "You seem to be enjoying all the activity around here, and a lot of these truckers seem to know you."

"They're just your average friendly trucker and yes, I guess I am enjoying all the activity, and it sure seems to be making Lou happy."

Glancing toward Lou, "Yeah, I don't think I've ever seen him happier."

"Are you going to pick Tim up?"

"I'm just about to leave."

"Drive carefully, and I'll see you in a couple of hours."

"As she's going out the door, Cindy waves, "Bye."

Stoney is cleaning the trucks windows, when he notices Cindy hurrying toward him.

"I thought you left."

"No, that darn car of mine won't start. I think it's the battery."

Handing her his keys, "Here, take my truck. When I get through here, I'll have a look at your car."

Giving him a kiss on the cheek, "Thanks Stoney." And hurrying over to the old Chevy truck she drives off.

Stoney is working around his campsite, when he looks up and sees Cindy and Tim.

Tim's way out in front, running as fast as he can. Cindy is looking concerned and calling out, "Be careful."

But Tim's not about to slow down and waving his arms, as he gets closer,. "Hi Stoney… Hi." Tim's running so fast he doesn't have a chance to slow down until Stoney catches him under his arms and swings him around, raising him over his head. "Hi partner. I was wondering when you'd get here."

"We would have been here sooner, but mom said she had to stop and talk to the Doctor."

"Well I'm sure that was important. Right?"

"Yeah, I guess so." And looking around, "Is that Roamer?"

"That's him" Setting him down, "Come on over and I'll introduce you."

"He sure is big. But how do you catch him?"

"Can you whistle?'

Looking a little doubtful, "Yeah… But not very good."

"Well how about if I help? Ready?" As Tim nods and tries to whistle, Stoney helps. Roamer raises his head and trots over to the camp, stopping just outside the campsite.

Cindy is standing back, a little apprehensive, watching as Tim and Stoney approach Roamer.

"Yeah he's big, but he's very gentle, especially around young cowboys."

"Can I pet him?"

As if understanding, Roamer puts his head down and nuzzles Tim's chest.

"He seems to like you."

Petting Roamers nose, "His nose sure is soft." Then, "I brought a couple of sugar cubes from the hospital, is it all right if I give them to Roamer?"

"Sure it's all right, and I'll bet he loves them. Just put one in your hand and hold your hand out with your palm flat, and let him take them out of your hand," Stoney tells him and watches as Timmy does as he was told.

Roamer sniffs them, and then gently takes them from Tim's outstretched palm.

"There, see how easy that was?"

"Yeah, he sure is gentle…. Can I ride him?"

"Are you ready?'

Tim is nodding his head as Stoney picks him up and swings him up on Roamer's back.

"Just hold on to his mane and Roamer will take you for a little ride around the camp."

"Don't I need a saddle or something?"

"Not with Roamer, he won't let anything happen to you. I'll walk along his side until you feel a little more comfortable. Okay?"

Tim nods his head again, and Roamer starts walking slowly with Stoney walking by their side. As they get around the camp to where Cindy's standing, chewing on her lower lip. "Okay cowboy, your, doing great so I'll just step over here by your mom where we can watch you."

Noticing his Mom, "Look Mom, I'm riding Roamer, isn't he beautiful?"

"You're both beautiful." Then turning to Stoney and quietly. "Do you think he'll be all right?"

'He'll be fine, I wouldn't let him do anything that would hurt him, and Roamer will take good care of him. He's as safe as if he was riding a big rocking horse, so stop worrying, just sit down, have a cup of coffee and relax.

Sitting down in a folding canvas chair, "Yeah, I know you wouldn't let him be doing that if you thought he would get hurt."

Stoney, hands Cindy, a cup of coffee, while saying, "He'll be fine, and now would you like to try some of my home made cookies?"

"Do you mean, you actually bake cookies out here?"

"Of course I do, I just use that little reflector oven over there,. I made them to celebrate Tim's homecoming, and they are chocolate chip.

Taking two cookies, "Mmmmm, they are good, and I must say, you really are a man of many talents."

Watching Tim on Roamer circle the camp, "This is all he talked about on the way home."

"Horses are good therapy for all youngsters; they give them a real feeling of accomplishment and closeness to nature."

"Did you read that in a book somewhere?"

"No, my Grandfather taught me that."

"He sounds like a very wise man."

"He is that."

"You sound very proud of him."

"Yes I guess I am, as I am of all my family."

"Tell me about your mother."

Looking at her for a moment, "She's very tall and very gentle, with black hair as black and shiny as a raven's wing, almost to her waist. Some say she's regal looking, and to this I must agree, in more ways than one, as while my grandfather chooses to live in the old ways and my father the new, it is really my mother who guides them both with her love and understanding."

"She sounds very beautiful.'

Thinking about his Mother, he nods. "Yes, she is very beautiful."

As she's watching Tim riding Roamer, "Are you sure he doesn't need a bridle?"

Smiling, "He'll be alright; Roamer knows where he's going."

And watching her son, with tears in her eyes, "I just wish he could always be this happy

"You know what I told you about your wishes. Now tell me what the Doctor said."

Taking a deep breath and exhaling slowly, "It wasn't good news. The Doctor told me that even after everything we've done, nothing has seemed to help. His white blood count is still extremely high and, besides the unlikely possibility of this going into remission, the only thing that could save him would be a bone marrow transplant, and finding a match at best is remote."

"How much time do they have to find a match?"

Slowly shaking her head, "Only until Timmy gets too weak to undergo a transplant operation, and that depends on how fast it progresses. It could be weeks, months, or even just a matter of a few days. He said when that happens, all they can do is try to make him as comfortable as possible."

"Does Tim know this?"

Cindy nods her head as tears come to her eyes. "I was thinking about what the Doctor said as I was bringing him home and I guess I started crying... Tim put his arms around me and said... Don't worry Mom, I know I'm going to be with Dad, but don't feel bad, I'll be all right..."

"But it is possible, that it could go into remission?"

"Yes it's possible, but the chances of that happening are very, very slim... And look at him riding that horse, he looks just like any other kid, without a worry in the world."

"You're right and he is brave, but even more important, he has faith."

Shaking her head and waving her hand in front of her eyes.. "Whee, that's enough of that; I'll go crazy if I keep thinking about it." Then looking at Tim. "You don't think he's getting too tired, do you?"

Stoney stands and walks over to the edge of the campsite, and Roamer immediately walks over to him. Taking Tim by the arms, Stoney lifts him off and sets him on the ground.

"Okay partner that's enough for now, let's let Roamer and your Mom rest a little, while we have a cookie."

Tim runs to his Mom and excitedly asks, "Did you see me Mom? Did you see me riding Roamer?"

"I saw you honey, you looked beautiful" And handing him some cookies. "Have some of these cookies, Stoney made them especially for you. And I want you to calm down. Remember what the Doctor told you."

Taking a few cookies he turns to Stoney. "Is this your camp?"

"This is it."

Looking around, "It's awesome." Then "Where do you sleep?

"Right over there in that bedroll."

"What if it rains?"

"Well it usually doesn't rain this time of the year, but if it did, I'd just put up a little tent."

Laughing, Cindy says. "Boy I wish I'd have thought of that. We could have got a tent."

"Yeah Mom, that would be cool."

Laughing, "No, I think you mean cold."

Grabbing another handful of cookies, "Can I go down by the water?"

Cindy glances at Stoney, who nods.

"All right, but be careful." Then, explaining to Cindy, "It's not very deep. The most he could do would be to get his feet wet." Then, asking, "Now tell me about yourself, why are you here working for Lou?"

Thinking about his question for a minute, "I don't really know. I went to school to become an accountant. Then when Jim died, I just pulled up stakes and wound up here, I didn't think my old car would take us much further, and I took this job with Lou because it gave me more time to spend with Timmy."

"What about your family?"

"I've been an orphan since I was eight and then I was raised by an alcoholic, abusive Aunt. It was all verbal abuse, but more than I could put up with, so I left as soon as I graduated from high school." Laughing, "When you think about it, I guess I haven't really had a life except for Timmy, and now I'm afraid I'm going to lose him."

"It sounds to me like you've had more than your share of problems, but what you've endured appears to have created a very beautiful, loving, strong willed, independent woman."

Laughing, "Is that supposed to be some kind of compliment?"

"It most assuredly is."

"Well, not that I don't like complements, but did you get a chance to look at my car?"

"Yes and you were right, it was the battery. I pulled it out of your car and put it on the charger in the garage."

"Thanks, and speaking of cars, I turned the radio on in your truck as I was driving into the hospital. But it wasn't a radio, it was a CB and it was tuned to channel 17, the truckers channel and a lot of the guys were calling for someone called Cherokee, like, Hey Cherokee, you out there? Or, Hey Cherokee, you got your ears on? Now you wouldn't happen to know who they might be calling, would you?"

Looking a little sheepish, "Well I suppose it could be almost anyone."

"Well I suppose it was you, and unless I'm greatly mistaken I think you've been on that CB telling all the truckers about the great food they are serving at Lou's Diner."

Laughing, "Well you're partly right."

"What do you mean, partly right?"

"I've also been telling them about "the Great View.""

"And just where is there a great view around here?"

"Now don't take this wrong, but in CB talk the views Great," means, the waitress is pretty."

"Oh my god, I don't believe this."

"You aren't mad at me are you?"

"No, of course not, I just think it's kind of funny." Then, "In this CB talk, what does Cotton Picker mean?"

"That's just a kind of endearment used between truckers. Why?"

"As some of the truckers have been leaving the diner they've been saying, See Ya on the Flip Side Cotton Picker, and I didn't understand what they meant."

"See Ya on the Flip Side, means they'll see you on their return trip."

"Yeah, well I heard this one on your CB this afternoon, one of them told another trucker that he had a Fat Load. Then the other guy said he had a load of Go Go Girls, then he told the trucker with the fat load that he better Do It, To It. What does that mean?"

"When a trucker says he's got a Fat Load, that means he's over the legal load limit. When the other driver told him to Do It to It, He meant he should Put the Petal to the Metal, meaning he better hurry before the county sheriff stopped him. And the guy with the load of Go Go Girls was saying he was carrying a load of cows or pigs to market."

"My god, they've got a language all their own."

"They sure have, and what I've told you is only part of it. Next time I go into town, I'll pick up a book on CB talk for you. It will probably come in handy, especially since I'm trying to talk Lou into letting me install a CB in the Diner. I think the truckers would like that, and it would even let a trucker who's running a little behind schedule place his dinner order before he even arrives at the diner."

"Where are all these truckers coming from?"

"Everywhere, however a lot of them are coming from the reservation."

"Why the reservation?"

"The reservation is involved in all kinds of industries including oil and natural gas exploration, uranium mining, coal mining, copper mining and logging to mention just a few, so there are always a lot of trucks coming and going from the reservation."

"I thought a lot of them looked like Native Americans." Then looking at Stoney, "And you thought by getting on the

CB, you'd be able to talk some of them into stopping in to have something to eat?"

"Yeah, but I got the idea from you, when you said you wished more truck drivers would stop at the diner. I thought I'd give it a try."

"Well it sure worked, they used to just drive on by and honk their horns once in awhile, but now they stop and that's great. Have you told Lou?"

"No and I hope you won't tell him either, let him think they're stopping because of his great cooking."

"I think you're probably right, the better he thinks his cooking is, the more pride he'll take in his cooking and the better it will become."

Turning to watch Tim play in the water, "I guess I better get him home and give him a nice hot bath."

"I'll walk you home."

Walking down to the stream, Stoney picks Tim up and sets him on Roamer's back. "Mom say's its time to go home, so Roamer's going to give you a ride home. Maybe we can do this again tomorrow."

"Can we Mom? Can we?"

"We'll see."

As their walking toward the cabins, "Thanks again Stoney, Thanks for everything, but mainly for just being a friend,"

"You don't have to thank me for anything, I enjoy being with you and Tim."

Roamer stops in front of Cindy's cabin, and Stoney lifts Tim off.

"Okay partner, get lots of rest tonight and I'll see you tomorrow." Then turning to Cindy, "Goodnight, and I'll see you in the morning."

"Goodnight Stoney."

Going back to his camp, feeling helpless, Stoney sits by the fire for hours, hoping for a sign that will tell what he is supposed to do about a little kid with leukemia.

**You don't make friends for the color of their skin, you
make friends for the goodness in their heart.**

13

Little Cotton Picker

Cindy has the coffee on and has already turned Lou's grill on when Stony arrives and is heading for the front door when she sees Lou arriving.

Calling out, to Lou, "These guys have been standing out there in the cold for over forty minutes, waiting for us to open." Stoney looks out in the parking area and sees four or five 18-wheelers sitting there with their engines idling, while their drivers are standing around talking. Cindy unlocks the front door and throwing it open, hollers to the drivers.

"Hey you cotton picker's better get in here where it's warm an have a hot cup of coffee on the house."
Stoney's grinning from ear to ear as he watches the drivers bust out in laughter. Still laughing as they walk in the door one big Navajo turns to Cindy smiling. "Cotton Pickers are we, well you better feed us Cotton Pickers some big breakfasts, Little Cotton Picker, cause we've been on the road a long time an we're mighty hungry."

As the big trucker is leaving, he turns to Cindy while smiling. "Be seeing you on the flip side Little Cotton Picker" It didn't take long for Cindy's new handle, *Little Cotton Picker* to get on the airwaves, and from then on Cindy became known as Little Cotton Picker and has really began to enjoy her new role.

Later in the day, she notices a trucker arrive with a load of cows. Waiting until he was seated and speaking loud enough to be heard by and for the amusement of the other truckers she asks, "Where are you taking your load of Go Go Girls?"

Then still later, when a trucker arrived with a flatbed rig loaded to the max with drilling pipe, she says, "Looks like you got a Fat Load there, better not let no County Mounty come up your back door, an you sure better stay away from those Chicken Coops."

To which he replies, "That's a Big Ten Four, Little Cotton Picker. But those Super Troopers got them Portable Chicken Coops now, an their kind of hard to stay away from, but when I leave here you can bet I'll be keepin my Eyeballs Peeled, the Pedal to the Metal, an be Doing it to it…"

"Well just be sure you keep your Shiny Side up and your Dirty Side down, an on your Flip I'll buy you a Mug of Motor Oil."

Sally who had been listening asked, "What was all that about?"

"Nothing much, I just told him I thought his truck was overloaded, and for him to be careful of the County Sheriff, and to stay away from truck weigh stations. Then he told me he knew, but was worried more about the State Troopers and their portable weigh stations, and when he leaves here, he's going to hurry and get rid of the overload as fast as possible. Then I told him to drive careful, and I'd buy him a cup of coffee when he got back this way." Then looking at Sally, with a straight face, "Are you telling me you didn't understand our conversation?"

Shaking her head while watching the trucker get up from the table, leaving a three-dollar tip on the table for Cindy, "No I sure didn't, but you can bet I'm going to learn to talk that way real soon."

Putting her arm around her friend as they walk toward the counter, "Well, I'll tell you what; I've got a little book under that counter over there that will tell you how. Only don't let these guys see you reading it, they might laugh. Besides, this

kind of talk has to sound kind of natural." Walking behind the
counter, Cindy bends down and lifts her sweater, showing
Sally where she put the book Stoney gave her. "Take it home
with you tonight, and I'll guarantee you'll be a new woman by
tomorrow morning."

"Yeah, well I'll settle for a new man."

Waving her hand as if to encompass the entire dining room.
"Take your pick honey."

Grinning, "Yeah, I might just do that."

"Okay now that we've got the lonely hearts stuff out of the
way, back to business. I've been talking to Lou about
changing the hours we're open. He's agreed to open an hour
earlier and to stay open an hour longer. I've made up a
tentative schedule for us, and I would like to see what you
think about it. This is just for you, Darlene, and myself. I still
don't know what we're going to do about Lou or Stoney yet.
In fact, I don't even know if Stoney will still be here after the
rodeo."

Looking at Cindy, "You kind of like him don't you?"

"Yeah, I guess I do, but I'm a big girl and I'll get over it."

Stoney is applying saddle soap to his bronc saddle when
Tim comes running into his camp.

"Where's your mom?"

Motioning over his shoulder, "She's coming."

"Oh, I see her now. I guess girls just don't walk as fast as
boys do."

"No, Mom walks pretty fast I just run faster."

Cindy walks into camp laughing, "I heard that young man,
and if I wasn't so tired from working all day I'd race you right
now."

Then noticing Stoney's bronc saddle, Tim asks. "Why does
that saddle look so funny?"

"Probably because it doesn't have a saddle horn."

"Why doesn't it have a saddle horn?"

Feeling he might upset Tim with the correct answer to his question. "Because a bronc rider isn't supposed to touch either his saddle or its horn with his hand when he's riding broncs."

Cindy's shaking her head. "And probably because the horn would hurt the cowboy if the horse happens to roll over on the cowboy."

"Well, the horse isn't supposed to roll over on the cowboy.'

"But it does happen."

"Yes it has been known to happen." And putting his bronc saddle up. "Now can we change the subject?"

Smiling,"Yeah, I'd like that."

Not understanding the by play between Stoney and his mother, Tim asks, "Can I ride Roamer again?"

"What do you think Mom, was he good and did he get lots of rest like he promised?"

"I'd say he was exceptionally good. He went right to bed after his bath and picked up his dirty clothes this morning, and even ate all his dinner this evening."

"Yeah, I'd say that was being real good. Okay partner are you ready to whistle?"

Before either of them, could whistle, Roamer walks up to the camp.

"Well, will you look at that? Roamer is as anxious as you are to go for a ride."

Picking Tim up, he places him on Roamer's back.

"All right partner here you go. Just remember to hold on to Roamer's mane."

After Tim rides off on Roamer, Stoney and Cindy walk slowly to the stream, where they sit on a large rock and watch the happy little kid on the great big gentle horse.

Cindy picks up a few pebbles and watches the ripples they make as she tosses them one at a time into the pool of water, then waits for the ripples to subside before tossing another pebble into the pool.

"I'm sorry Stoney."

"Sorry for what."

"Oh, a lot of things, but just now for the way I reacted over your bronc saddle. I shouldn't have remarked about it the way I did, especially in front of Tim. It's just that I can't understand why you guys do those dumb kinds of things." Glancing at Stoney, "I guess down deep it reminds me of Jim."

"Yes, I imagine it would resurrect some unpleasant memories, and I want you to know I'll understand if you change your mind about going tomorrow."

"No, I really want to go..." With a glistening of tears in her eyes, Cindy continues, "Jim loved the thrill and excitement of rodeo, while I was always scared to death of them. In fact in all the time Jim rode, I never once went to watch him ride, I was that scared, but I refused to admit it to either Jim or to myself. I always managed to find an excuse for not going with him; either the baby or I weren't feeling well or I couldn't find a baby sitter... So yes, I very much want to go because tomorrow, in my heart, through you I'll be seeing Jim riding out there and maybe, just maybe it will help me understand. Or if not understand, at least accept Jim's, ... for lack of a better word, love affair with rodeo." Standing up and taking Stoney's hand. "Come on, lets see if you have any coffee left in that old pot."

Stoney builds up the fire and putting the coffee pot over the fire for a few minutes, warms the coffee up.

"If you'd rather have a soft drink or some juice, I've got some in the ice chest?" "Thanks but coffee sounds fine, and the stronger the better."

Sitting back drinking their coffee they watch Tim riding Roamer, when Cindy asks, "How did you get started riding rough stock?"

Thinking back and chuckling to himself, "Well I think I must have been about Timmy's age."

Interrupting, "You're kidding."

"No, I couldn't have been more than six, but it wasn't really rough stock I was riding, it was sheep."

Almost laughing, "Sheep?"

Grinning, "Yeah sheep, they called it Mutton Bustin. It was at a local rodeo, and boy was I ever scared. There were a lot of us little guys and they put helmets on us, something like football helmets and pads on our knees and elbows and then they picked me up and sat me down in this little chute on this little black faced sheep." Shaking his head as he remembers, "I was scared to death, and when they opened the gate and that little sheep came bounding out of that chute with me on his back, boy I was even more scared. I was holding on for all I was worth,. but I only lasted for about three hops and I was sitting in the dust on my fanny, and everyone was laughing.

But I can still remember that little sheep with his black face turning around and looking at me, kind of like he was saying, that'll teach you.

I jumped up and ran back to that chute as fast as I could run, and actually pushed the next kid out of my way so I could climb up on the chute and get on that next little sheep, that was baaing his head off as I climbed on him, and sat waiting for the chute to open.

All the cowboys standing around were having a good old time laughing at me. But someone finally reached over and opened the chute, and when they did me and that little sheep came out of that chute like we were one. I stayed on that little sheep until the little guy was just too tired to buck anymore.

From then on I was hooked, I'd ride anything I could get a rope on calves, heifers, steers, horses and by the time I was twelve I was riding bulls."

"And you've never been hurt?"

"Oh, I've been tossed around a bit, but nothing serious, a few cracked ribs now and then, and a broken arm or two."

"Yeah that confirms it, you're crazy."

Laughing, "Not really Cindy, not when you consider that life itself is a risk, and if you sit home with the covers pulled up over your head all the time you'll never enjoy life. I believe you have to take risks now and then to make life worthwhile."

"But you'll last longer, without risk," Looking at her son. "Maybe."

Changing the subject, "I picked up some marshmallows today. I thought Tim would like to roast some over the fire this evening."

"I'll bet he would, I don't think he's ever roasted marshmallows on an open fire."

"And I've got another surprise for him."

"What kind of surprise."

"When we were talking the other evening you remarked that Timmy was only half Navajo. I told you that even if he only had one drop of Indian blood, he was Indian, and because I feel it's important Native Americans never forget their wonderful heritage I made a pair of moccasins for Timmy. I hope you don't mind."

"Of course I don't mind, but do you mean you actually made a pair of moccasins yourself?"

"Of course."

"May I see them?"

Removing a small pair of moccasins from his bedroll, he hands them to Cindy.

As she examines them, "They're beautiful and so soft, how in the world did you ever learn to do something like this?"

"My grandfather taught me. I've been making my own moccasins since I was ten."

"How did you know his size?"

"I made them a little large, but when they get wet from either the grass or the stream, they'll shrink as they dry to the exact size and shape of his foot."

"He's going to love them." Then "This reminds me. When I see you running in the morning, I see you wearing a colored headband. I always thought headbands were supposed to be leather."

"Prior to the early seventeen hundreds the Cherokee wore their hair in a Mohawk, that is, shaved on both sides with the center strip of hair about three inches long standing straight up, with a long thatch of hair hanging from the back of their heads almost to their waist."

Interrupting, "They must have looked very fierce."

"In fact they were extremely fierce. Then in the early seventeen hundreds, the Cherokee Nation signed a treaty with the English, and the English were so happy about this treaty they insisted on taking a delegation of Cherokees to England to meet their Queen. However when they arrived there, the Lords of England thought the Cherokee were too savage looking for them to present to their Queen, so they took the turbans from their own servants who were from India, and dressed the Cherokee in turbans to make them look more presentable for the Queen. The Cherokee delegation liked the turbans so much, they insisted on keeping them. When they returned home wearing their bright colored turbans they were met with overwhelming acceptance by the entire Cherokee Nation, and to this day Cherokee wear colored turbans.

The small band I wear is known as a small turban, while many Cherokee still wear the full turban."

"You mean to say the Cherokee actually got their first turbans from the English, because some Lords thought the Queen might be offended by their appearance?"

"Yes."

"That's amazing, and to think your heritage goes back to the early seventeen hundreds."

Laughing, "I'm afraid it goes back many thousands of years before that."

"That... That would be before the birth of Christ."

Smiling, "Yes, at least twelve thousands of years before."

Shaking her head, "Yes, I can see now why you would be very proud of your heritage."

"Tim should also be proud of his heritage for the Navajo have been able to survive some of the worst atrocities imagined by man."

"What sort of atrocities?"

Hesitantly, "The Navajo have always been a very peaceful, ambitious people who didn't take part in the so-called Indian wars, unless pushed. They were one of the first tribes to accept the way of the immigrant settlers, the first to accept cotton clothing, and their way of farming. The Navajo had vast herds of sheep and many cattle. Only many in power still considered them savages.

The Army built Fort Defiance, taking much of the Navajo grazing land for the grazing of Army horses. This set off a powder keg, resulting in Navajo raids on the Army and Army raids on the Navajo.

A thousand Navajo warriors launched an attack on Fort Defiance, causing the Army to abandon Fort Defiance. Then in retaliation, the Army launched an aggressive attack on the Navajo, burning crops, and slaughtering and confiscating livestock to such an extent the Navajo faced starvation.

A peace agreement was signed in 1861 including an agreement where the government would supply much needed supplies to replace what they had destroyed and confiscated.

When the supplies where finally brought to the Navajo after many months of false promises and delays The Navajo began a celebration, feasting, dancing and a day of horse racing, and of course the Army was invited to join in. Everyone was enjoying the festivities; the Navajo won some of the horse races and the Army won some.

Everyone was enjoying themselves, until the very last race of the day, when one of the soldiers out and out cheated, and his Commander laughingly declared him the winner, in spite of his cheating. The Navajo could not understand this and a minor altercation occurred. The Commander ordered his detachment to open fire on the Navajo, killing over 30 Navajo, men women and children. This of course ended any thought of peace and the Navajo retaliated with attacks of their own.

In 1863, the Army sent Colonel Christopher "Kit" Carson on his scorched earth mission against the Navajo. They stormed into the ancient and sacred Canyon de Chelly, killing and butchering Navajo by the hundreds, burning their Hogan's, slaughtering their livestock, and burning their crops including an estimated two million pounds of corn. Kit Carson, who to this very day is portrayed as a hero by Hollywood and the media, allowed his command to butcher and slaughter unarmed women and children. Even allowing them to amuse themselves by raping captured and even wounded Navajo women, amusing themselves to the extent they were playing catch with the severed breasts of young Navajo women.

After rounding up their captives and keeping them in imprisonment for months on near starvation diets, the Army forced these 8,000 Navajo, men women and children on a grueling three hundred and sixty mile trek across New Mexico's most desolate, treacherous desert. Young and old men, chained together, urged on by rifle butts and whips across a scorching hot desert, Women and children following behind, herded like a herd of cattle. Hundreds dropping like flies from dehydration and heat exhaustion. This herding of human beings by the U.S. Army, has since, become known as "The Long Walk." A walk to hell, a walk to a dry sun baked, unforgiving piece of land known as Bosque Renondo, which became the first concentration camp, the world has ever seen. What little water was available was alkali water, almost too bitter to drink, and the ground too rocky for crops. Without enough firewood for either cooking or warmth in the freezing winters, hundreds died from the cold and malnutrition.

All this occurred at a time when slaves were supposedly, being set free across our nation. Yet the United States Army enslaved their Navajo captives and forced them to mold adobe bricks to build Fort Sumner, under conditions so horrible the Navajo began to perish in such great numbers that even the Army was unable to keep it quiet. Hearing of this atrocity, churches throughout the land began an uproar, which eventually, was taken up by the Newspapers until Congress, afraid of losing votes, were forced to order the Navajo released and allowed to return to their homes. They set these Navajo free, with nothing except what clothing they had on their backs, to make another Long Walk across some of New Mexico's harshest terrain in the dead of summer where temperatures exceeded 110 degrees. In all the Navajo lost over four thousand of their people. This was more than half of their entire population. But they never lost heart, they never lost their dignity and they never lost their pride of being Navajo."

Spellbound and unashamed of the tears running down her cheeks, "This can't be true; no one could be that cruel to another human being."

Slowly shaking his head, Stoney replies, "I only wish I could tell you it never happened, but it did." Wiping tears from her eyes, Cindy says, "Oh my god, I don't think I'll ever be able to look at another Navajo without feeling guilty."

"I don't think any Navajo would want you to feel guilty for something you had nothing to do with. I only hope when you next look at a Navajo you do so with a little understanding."

It is turning dusk as Stoney adds a few logs to the fire. "I think we should begin roasting marshmallows."

Stoney walks to the edge of the campsite and picks Tim up off Roamer's back. "Roamer's going to have a busy day tomorrow, so maybe we better let him get a little rest tonight and you'll be able to ride him a little tomorrow."

"Can I just pet him for awhile?"

Nodding approval, Stoney says, "When you're through petting him, we've got a surprise for you."

Walking back to the fire he sits down by Cindy. "He'll be here as soon as he finishes petting Roamer."

Receiving no response, he glances at Cindy and notices she is gazing at the Evening Star, and watching her lips he knows she is wishing on the stars. Not wanting to appear he's noticed, he adds another log to the fire and turns his attention to Tim as he approaches the fire.

Tim asks, "What's the surprise?"

"Well it's actually two surprises… First I want you to sit down here by your mom so she can try a new pair of shoes on you."

Sounding disappointed, Tim asks, "New shoes, that's the surprise?"

Holding up the moccasins, "But you've never had a pair of shoes like these." Cindy says.

Amazed, "Those aren't shoes, they're moccasins."

"You're right and Stoney made them especially for you, so you better sit down over here so we can see how they fit."

Cindy removes his regular shoes and slips the moccasins on and ties them with rawhide ties just above his ankles. Tim jumps up and runs around the campsite.

"Look, look Mom. I can run even faster."

"Yes you can, but I don't want you to get too tired so you better sit down for awhile and rest. Besides, I don't think I heard you thank Stoney yet."

Tim runs over and sits between his Mother and Stoney.

"Thanks Stoney, they're beautiful." Feeling the soft leather with his hand, and says, "I'll never take them off."

Cindy laughs. "That's what I'm afraid of."

"Well I think you better take them off once in awhile, at least long enough to wash your feet every now and then. Okay?"

Rubbing the soft deer skin of his new moccasins, Tim nods.

"And now for the other surprise," Stoney picks up a very slim, green cottonwood branch and, putting a marshmallow on its tip, hands it to Tim. "We're going to roast some marshmallows." Handing another one to Cindy, "Here Mom, show us how it's done."

Soon, they are all-roasting marshmallows over the campfire.

As traditional people, we believe we are one with our creator's creatures and one with our mother earth, who provides us with everything we need.

14

The Carnival

Early the next morning, Cindy, Tim and Stoney are in his old Chevy pickup pulling Roamer in the horse trailer down the 3-lane highway toward Riverton.

Yawning Cindy says, "I didn't know rodeos started so early."

"They don't, but we have to get there early so I have time to register and to make the draw."

"What's the draw?"

"Every contestant participates in a drawing to determine what rough stock he's going to ride."

"Does it really make a difference?"

"All the deference in the world… Bronc riding and bull riding events are judged on a point system. The judges award points on the performance of both the rider and the animal, a possible fifty points for the rider and another possible fifty points for the animal.

So it's extremely important to draw a bucking horse or a bull that's going to give it everything it's got. Otherwise a good rider on a not so good animal doesn't really have much of a chance of winning."

"So what you're saying is the more vicious and the more your horse or bull bucks, the better your chance of winning is."

"That's close, but a good rider can also help his horse or bull perform to his maximum abilities."

Shaking her head in disbelief, "I knew it… You guys are all nuts."

Sitting on his mom's lap, Tim asks. "What are you going to ride, a bull or a horse?"

"Probably both."

"Far out."

"And it's even contagious." Cindy says, shaking her head.

As they turn into the fairgrounds. "Look Mom a merry-go-round."

"Oh, they must be having a carnival, and look there's a Ferris wheel. Doesn't it look like fun?" Pausing then, "I haven't been to a carnival in years."

"Well we can fix that. Just give me enough time to get Roamer taken care of and signed in. Then we should have plenty of time for the carnival."

"Oh, boy… Can I go on the merry-go-round?"

"Sure you can, and we might even be able to talk your mom into going on the merry-go-round."

"You guys don't have to worry about me; I'm an old hand at merry-go rounds. I'll show you both how to ride."

After finding an empty paddock for Roamer and seeing he has fresh water and a good ration of oats and hay. Stoney asks an old wrangler for directions to the rodeo office, and hires him to watch over roamer, until they get back from the carnival.

. Leaving Cindy and Tim looking over the Brahma bulls and broncs in the pens directly behind the bucking chutes, he goes to register for the rodeo.

The rodeo office, like most of the other offices at the fair grounds, old and almost wore out, due to lack of county funding.

But none of the other cowboys already there, waiting to sign up for the various events, seem to notice the well worn wooden floor with gaps between a few of the floorboards or the almost solid mass of spider webs in the exposed beamed ceiling.

Picking up an entry form and studying the events while standing in line Stoney notices a weathered faced cowboy, who ambles over.

Hayes Carlin, honest looking with that self-determined rugged look that comes from a life of hard work, dark hair with a touch of silver at his temples, and wearing well-worn jeans and boots, and a western hat even more beat up than Stoney's.

Asking, "Didn't I see you do a little riding up Oklahoma way?"

Looking at this cowboy, Stoney thinks he looks a little familiar, then immediately dismisses the thought.

"Yeah, I've done some riding up that way."

And with a grin Stoney likes immediately. "I thought so, and if my memory serves me right I'd say these boys around here are in for a little competition today."

"Well I don't know about that, but thanks for the thought. Are you riding today?"

Almost sadly, shaking his head, "No, I'm getting a little too old for the rough stock; it takes too long for me to heal these days. But I still like to hang around and think about the good old days."

"You don't strike me as being too old to ride anything they've got around here."

"Thanks son, that kind of talk always makes me feel a lot younger. What events are you figuring on entering?

"I thought I might try, calf roping, both bare and saddle bronc, and the bulls.

"It sounds like you've got a pretty full day planed for yourself."

Unnoticed by Stoney, Cliff Walker and another younger cowboy have entered and are standing directly behind him.

Cliff interrupts their conversion with a laugh, "The Chief doesn't stand a chance, an if he had any sense at all he'd just save his money an go on home."

Stoney ignores Cliff's remark; Hayes doesn't and looking Cliff in the eye, says, "Well if I was a betting man, I think I'd put my money on him." Turning back to Stoney, "You know in order to qualify for all around, you have to enter five events, and if you just happened to enter steer wrestling, I'd consider it an honor to haze for you."

Looking in his new friends sparkling blue eyes, "You know I think I'd like that. But why don't we go all the way?"

"What you got in mind?"

"How are you with a rope?"

Smiling from ear to ear. "Fair son, fair to middlin."

"Then I think I'll just sign us up for a little team roping too."

Chuckling, Hayes says, "I've got a feeling this is going to be a good day."

After showing their PRCA *"Professional Rodeo Cowboys of America"*, cards, Stoney signs up for all six events. After Stoney arranges to meet Hayes for the Grand Entry, he goes back to the stock pens where he finds Cindy and Tim feeding handfuls of grass to the Brahma bulls.

In a teasing kind of voice, Cindy says, "Heck these guys are so gentle; I bet I could even ride them."

"Yeah, well don't let that gentle nature of theirs fool you, they're just resting there thinking about all the bad things they are going to do to all us unsuspecting young cowboys."

Anxiously, Tim asks, "Can we go to the carnival now?"

Putting his hand on Tim's shoulder, "We sure can, and let's go to the merry-go-round first and see who's got the fastest horse."

The music of a carrousel is always enough to lighten the heart and bring the little kid out in anyone.

Tim's holding on to the shiny metal pole supporting his little wooden horse with all his might, as his horse goes round and round and up and down. Laughing and hollering to Stoney. "We all have the fastest horse."

"I wouldn't be too sure of that; look at your Mom, her horse must be going faster than ours."

Cindy's riding like she's a jockey coming down the home stretch. Tim is still laughing when they get off the merry-go-round and sees someone selling cotton candy.

"Look mom, cotton candy."

"Do you want some?"

"Please."

Cindy and Tim are eating their cotton candy, waiting for Stoney to get his when Tim says, "It's kind of like eating air"

As he's about to take another bite Cindy gently pushes his hand, causing his nose to go into the cotton candy.

"But it's a lot stickier than air, and now you've got a pink nose."

Wiping his nose on his shirtsleeve, Tim asks, "Is it really pink?"

"Hey I saw that and you better not even think about trying that on me." Stoney says

"Spoil sport."

They wander through the carnival eating their cotton candy, pausing every once in awhile to watch the action at the various arcades, even stopping to watch some jugglers perform.

Stoney and Tim try their luck at throwing baseballs at some rag dolls sitting on rows of shelves, winning a couple of stuffed animals for Cindy. Then they ride the Ferris Wheel with Tim in the center holding on for dear life. Then have some soft drinks and mile long hotdogs, with Stoney having two. Which they eat while standing in front of an arcade with a huge banner advertising the tattooed lady and a two headed calf, which everyone decides they don't want to see.

Noticing Stoney glance at his watch and sensing he's anxious and yet not wanting to end Tim's enjoyment, Cindy suggests, "Maybe we should start back for the rodeo arena so we can get Roamer ready for the grand entry."

Roamer is enjoying all the attention he's getting with Stoney cleaning his hoofs, while Cindy and Tim give him a good brushing.

After checking his bronc saddle and bull rope again, Stoney bridles and saddles Roamer, then checks his catch rope and ties it to his saddle. Picking Tim up Stoney sets him in the saddle before they start for the arena, where luckily they find some front row seats for Tim and Cindy in the stands closest to the bucking chutes.

And of course they're closest to and down wind of the stock pens, and Cindy soon discovers why these stands are usually occupied by the participant's family, friends, and other animal lovers. "Wheeh, the air around here sure adds to the atmosphere."

Still sitting on Roamer, Tim sniffs the air, "I think it smells kind of neat."

Laughing, "I think he's been hanging around Lou's kitchen too long."

Shaking his head, "That's not very nice."

"No, you're right and I apologize I should have said how Lou's kitchen used to smell."

"You're impossible."

Hayes rides up, mounted on a big Buckskin gelding, and Stoney makes the introductions. After tipping his hat to Cindy and shaking Tim's hand, he says. "I thought I'd ride over to let you know they're starting to form up for the grand entry."

"I'm ready." With Cindy, at his side and with Hayes and Tim both mounted, they walk over to where the participants are gathering. As they pass some mounted riders, Cindy notices Cliff Walker, who smiles and touches the brim of his hat as a sign of acknowledgement.

Thinking he might not have noticed, she squeezes Stoney's hand and quietly. "There's Cliff, I knew he'd be here."

Not even glancing at Cliff. "Yeah, we met earlier today."

Before they get too far in among the horses Stoney stops, and helping Tim off Roamer, sets him on the ground. "Now I want you to watch out for your mom, and be sure she gets back to our seats safely and I'll bring Roamer back to you in a few minutes. okay?"

"Okay Stoney, I'll take care of her." Taking his mother's hand, Tim says, "Come on mom, and be careful."

Cindy is smiling over her shoulder at Stoney as she lets Tim lead the way back to their seats.

Mounting Roamer, he and Hayes join the other riders forming a line two abreast behind the mounted flag bearers.

Live life as if everyday was a new adventure

15

The Rodeo

The announcer is explaining. "The art of rodeo began over a hundred and fifty years ago. It began when cowboys all across our great nation. Cowboys of all colors; black, yellow, brown, red, and white, would come together to gather or herd cattle.

Like little boys, who many of them at that time were, some only twelve and thirteen years old, they couldn't resist the opportunity to display their riding and roping abilities, abilities they needed in their everyday lives just to stay alive.

This evolved into rodeo as it is today, and I would like to remind you that what you will be witnessing here today is an art. An art that has been perfected over those hundred and fifty years, by cowboys who have honed their skill to perfection, cowboys and cowgirls, who still put their lives at risk every time they throw a leg over one of these animals… Now let's welcome them with a big round of applause."

The gate is swung open and, to recorded music, the grand entry begins, led by two very attractive young women mounted on their beautiful immaculately groomed horses, carrying both the New Mexico State flag and the Stars and Stripes. Followed by twenty or thirty other young women, all in brightly colored western outfits, mounted on their magnificent mounts, followed by forty or fifty cowboys, young and old, mostly wearing clean but well-worn working western outfits.

The spectators stand in reverent silence as our flag passes, men with their hats over their hearts. Then, they clap and cheer as they watch the procession of cowboys and cowgirls pass, waving to family, friends, and all the many children in attendance. The riders make two rounds of the arena, before forming a double line down the center of the arena facing the flag bearers, who have turned their horses to face the assembled group of spectators in the stands.

The cowboys remove their hats and place them over their hearts, as an old bowlegged cowboy steps forward to sing our National Anthem in such a deep resonating voice that it sends shivers up the backs of everyone in attendance.

At its conclusion, the flag bearers turn their mounts and make another full circle of the arena at a gallop with everyone following, before exiting.

Stoney and Hayes ride their mounts over to where Cindy and Tim are sitting and as Stoney dismounts, Hayes remarks "We've got a little time before steer wrestling, so I think I'll just wander around and talk to a few old friends. I'll meet you at the chutes after you ride your bronc."

Nodding, "That'll work." Then turning, he sets Tim in the saddle and asks, "Think you can take care of Roamer while I sit with your Mom for awhile?"

"You bet."

The announcer seems to keep up a running dialog. "Thank you, thank you, and now let's give them all a big round of applause."

As the fans are applauding, several cowboys roll three barrels into the arena, which they place standing on end, one barrel on each side of the arena and one at the far end. Two others are setting a timing device up about five feet in front of the gate.

The announcer explains.

"Our first event on this beautiful sunny afternoon will be barrel racing. This is a timed event, with the contestants racing through a timing light as they race into the arena as fast as their horse can run. They will first circle to the right, clockwise, around the first barrel. Then across the arena to the second barrel circling to the left, counter clockwise, then racing to the third barrel at the far end of the arena, which they will circle once again to the left, counter clockwise, and then race the full length of the arena at full speed, crossing the timing light again before exiting the arena.

Knocking a barrel over is a five second penalty, deducted from their overall time, and a rider is disqualified if they do not follow the specified cloverleaf pattern.

Some of these young ladies you will be seeing here this afternoon have been training both themselves and their horses for this event for years, and are rated as some of the best in the country. Many of these young women will be competing in Las Vegas, Nevada this December for the Grand National Barrel Racing Championship.

And if any of you have ever wondered why they put saddle horns on saddles, I think you'll have your answer when you see how fast some of these young ladies turn around these barrels.

And now for our first contestant, let's give a welcome to Carol Tober out of Reno Nevada, riding her horse Boomer."

There's a roar of applause as Carol, almost stretched out flat on her horses back, races her horse Boomer into the arena at full speed, passing through the timing light and heading to the first barrel. Making the turn around the first barrel, Boomer is leaning almost on his side. Coming out of his turn he straightens up and, stretching out as far as he can, Boomer races for the second barrel with Carol lying almost flat on his back, urging him on to even greater speed he races across the arena turning around the second barrel in a like manner. He is running full out for the last barrel at the far end of the arena.

Circling the barrel, with dirt flying and to the roar of the crowd, laying almost horizontal to the ground, but as he straightens up to make his dash for the finish line, Carols boot catches the top of the barrel, raising it up on edge.

The crowd Ohhhhs as the barrel wobbles back and forth, but it doesn't fall, with the crowd applauding and cheering them on. With Carol lying almost flat on his back, using her white hat to urge him on, Boomer races for the finish line.

Cindy is jumping up and down with excitement, watching this beautiful display of horsemanship and, without pausing to take a breath, "That was beautiful. I felt like I was almost afraid to breathe when that barrel started to tip over, and I never saw a woman ride like that before, and the outfit she was wearing was absolutely gorgeous."

Smiling to himself, "And the horse wasn't bad either."

Laughing, "You're right; the horse did his part too."

"Yeah, without the horse, she wouldn't have gotten to the first barrel."

"Oh, you men are all impossible. I was just so surprised to see a woman ride so well."

Laughing, "I was only kidding, and you shouldn't be surprised. These young women work hard at this and it is not easy. Like the man said, they work years at it and they take a lot of falls before they get as good as the young lady we just saw. And many of them have everything they own invested in their horse and rig, just so they can go down the road to the next rodeo."

"You make it sound like it's their life.'

"For many of them, that's exactly what it is. It's a hard life but they love it, they love every minute of it."

"Yes, I think I can understand that, and maybe I've complained too much about the life I've been dealt."

"Many of us complain too much about the cards we're dealt, but in your case I think you've had a few cards dealt from the bottom of the deck. Now if you'll excuse me, I better get ready for the bronc riding." Then looking at Tim on Roamer, he asks Cindy "Will you take care of Roamer until I get back."

Looking at her son sitting on roamer, patting his neck, "You don't have to worry about Roamer, he's in good hands."

Nodding, Stoney picks up his rough out bronc saddle and walks over to the bucking chutes where they have just started to move the broncs into the chutes.

Climbing up on one of the chutes, he helps one of the riders saddle his bronc, tighten the cinch, and settle into his saddle, while, the announcer is saying, "I hope you're ready for a thrill a minute, because our next event of the afternoon will be saddle bronc riding. Our first contestant coming out of chute number two, will be Ben Little Horn Rawlins off our own Navajo reservation just down the road apiece. Riding, Nightmare..."

Stoney asks. "Ready?"

Taking a firm grip on his rope and a deep seat in his saddle, Ben nods his head and says, "Let er go." As another cowboy snugs up the flank strap, the gate flies open. With eyes ablaze, Nightmare comes flying out of that chute, spinning to the left then dropping his head so fast Ben hasn't a chance of keeping it up, and he's pulled forward loosing his balance. Nightmare follows this with a series of tremendous bucks, dumping Ben Little Horn in the middle of the arena. Nightmare, still bucking, continues around the arena until one of the pickup riders is able to catch up to him to release his flank strap.

Announcer, in his deep raspy voice says. "No score for Ben Little Horn."

Looking a little unsteady, Ben tries to get up only to stagger and fall to his knees. Several cowboys jump off the bucking chutes, running into the arena to help, only to be waved off by Ben as he finally gets to his feet

Announcer. "Let's give that young man the kind of hand he deserves for a valiant effort." The crowd stands and cheers and Ben waves his hat in thanks as he hobbles out of the arena.

Stoney helps two more riders get their bronc saddles on and cinched up, only to watch their un-successful attempts.

When hearing the announcer say. "Our next contestant will be Cliff Walker out of Prescott Arizona riding Last Chance, out of chute #3, Stoney looks over, in time to see Cliff nod his head. And when the gate suddenly opens, Last Chance literally explodes out of the chute, with his ears pinned back, and his head down, bucking as high and as hard as he can. He comes down stiff legged, spinning to the right, and then takes off in a tremendous bucking run around the arena. The crowd is on their feet screaming their approval, as the eight-second horn sounds and watching the pickup riders move in to pick Cliff off the horse. Stoney is smiling to himself while thinking. This cowboy knows how to ride. Cliff slides off the pickup horse and, pleased with his ride, is smiling and waving his hat to the crowd as he walks back to the bucking chutes.

As the announcer is saying, "A good ride and a very respectable score of 76…. Now, are you ready for this? Our next rider is Jim Walker out of Prescott, Arizona riding Shoulda Walked, out of chute number 4. That's right folks, Cliff Walker's little brother is following in his big brothers footsteps."

Looking over Stoney watches as the young cowboy nods his head and the gate is thrown open, Shoulda Walked comes out of the chute in a series of stiff legged, twisting, hopping bucks, then suddenly spinning to the left, dumps Jim unceremoniously in the dirt. Getting up, Jim picks up his hat and, disgusted with his ride, uses his hat to dust the dirt off the seat of his pants.

Seeing his bronc move into the chute, Stoney begins to put his gear on the horse, as the announcer announces "No score on Walker." Our last contestant in our bronc-riding event will be Stoney Wood out of Oklahoma City, riding Widow Maker out of chute number 1. And he's a got a score of 76 to beat, a tough row to hoe."

Taking a deep seat and a tight grip on his rope, Stoney nods his head and says. "Let's go." As the gate is thrown open, the cowboy at the rear of the chute tugs the flank strap tight.

Widow Maker explodes out of the chute, with Stoney on his back straight up, twisting and turning, spinning to the right, then to the left, with Stoney working his spurs all the way, spurring from chest to flanks.

Widow Maker isn't giving an inch, his head is down and he's giving it everything he's got, but Stoney is sticking to him like glue. The crowd is on their feet, screaming and cheering, as the brave horse pours his heart into trying to unseat his rider with a hard bucking run across the arena.

The eight-second buzzer sounds and the pickup riders move in, but before they can get there, Stoney appears to lean forward, giving the horse a pat on its neck. Then leaping off, he hits the ground running.

As Stoney is walking back to the chutes, the Announcer says "As beautiful a ride as you're likely to see, and a score of 78.

Stoney waves to the crowd and, as he continues walking to the chutes he notices Cliff looking his way, with a smile and what appears to be a slight nod of his head.

Hayes Carlin jumps down from the chutes and slaps him on the back as he congratulates him on his great ride, while other cowboys are shaking his hand and slapping him on the back.

Hayes walks with Stoney toward the fence. "I think steer wrestling is up next."

"Then I better get Roamer."

"A friend is holding Lotta Bucks out behind the stands, so I'll walk over to the stands with you."

Tim sees Stoney and Hayes approaching, and begins waving and calling to Stoney before he even gets there.

When Stoney looks up, he is surprised to see both Cindy and
Tim on Roamer. Seeing the surprise in his eyes,
"I figured if those ladies could ride like that, I could at least
ride this big rocking horse around here."

Tim reaches out, wrapping his arms around Stoney's neck.
"I knew you could do it, I told mom you'd do it."

Lifting Tim off Roamer and high in the air while laughing,
"Well it's not over yet partner, let's wait and see how it all
comes out."

"You'll do it, you'll win, I know you'll do it."

"Well, I promise to do my best."

"Holding out her arms while smiling. "If you help me off,
I'll give you your horse back."

"That's a deal" and lifting Cindy down, "I sure hope you
haven't spoiled him because he's got a lot of work to do."

He is mounting Roamer just as Hayes, riding Lotta Bucks,
rides up. Tipping his hat to Cindy "Sorry folks, but I've got to
borrow this cowboy for a few minutes."

With a wink, "Just try to bring him back in one piece."

"Do my best ma'am."

Stoney and Hayes ride over by the gate, where they can
watch the wranglers herding the steers into a pen behind the
chute.

After examining the steers for a few minutes, Hayes off
handedly remarks, "They look a might big. and a little older
means a little wiser."

With a smile, "Worried?"

"Just for some of these young yahoos."

"My thoughts exactly."

16

Hayes Carlin

Announcing the next event, "Our next event of the afternoon will be steer wrestling and I might add this is definitely not for the faint of heart… Now for you first timers let me explain… This is a two-man operation, the dogger and the hazer… The hazer's job is to keep the steer running in a straight line, or at least as straight as possible, allowing the dogger to get in position, to leap from his horse, grabbing the steer by the horns and throwing the steer to the ground. All four legs must be pointing in the same direction… This is a timed event with the fastest time being the winner….

Stoney and Hayes sit on their horses and watch their competition. Two teams with a no score, one with a very acceptable 6.42.seconds

Announcing , "Our next contestants are Cliff Walker out of Prescott Arizona riding Amigo, and his Brother Jim Walker out of Prescott Arizona riding Little Man… And they have to beat six point four two seconds."

Cliff and Jim ride their horses into the starting box, backing them to the rear of the box, one on each side of the chute. They watch the steer in the chute. A cowboy has just set the timing barrier across the front of the starting box.

Their horses are nervous; Cliff and Jim, with their eyes
glued to the chute, see the chute suddenly fly open and, almost
as fast the steer dashes out, Cliff and Jim are spurring their
horses, racing after it...
Jim's keeping it from veering off to the right, as Cliff on
Amigo comes up on the steers left. Leaning off Amigo's right
Cliff reaches out, grabbing the steers horns. Leaping off his
horse, digging his heels into the soft dirt, braces his body, and
exerting all his strength, throws the steer to the ground.

With the crowd cheering, the judge lowers his flag...
Announcer, "Time... is five point three one... and you can
believe me folks, that is going to be hard to beat."

Smiling to himself, Stoney remarks, "Not bad."

Hayes shrugs his shoulders and with a smile, replies,
"Amateurs."
They watch another team compete.

Announcer, "Time six point four five seconds."

Turning Lotta Bucks toward the starting box. "We're up
next."

"Then let's do it."

Our next contestants will be Stoney Wood out of
Oklahoma City riding his big black and white stallion Roamer,
and his hazer is one of our all time old favorites, Hayes Carlin
out of Douglas, Arizona riding Lotta Bucks.

Stoney and Hayes ride their horses into the starting box and,
while their backing them to the rear of the box, Hayes
remarks, "We have to come out of here fast if we want to beat
em."

Stoney just nods his head.

Roamer and Lotta Bucks seem to know why they are there,
both tensing and flexing their muscles while watching the
steer in the chute with as much intensity as their riders.

The cowboy has set the timing barrier and tension builds,
when suddenly the gate flies open and the steer bolts out of the
chute as if his life depended on it.

The two great horses, seemingly anticipating the opening of the gate, are already running, exerting every muscle in their bodies. Just two leaps out of the box they are already coming along side the steer.

Stoney leans over and grabbing the steers horn, leaps off Roamer, swinging his feet forward, bracing his legs and digging his heels in while twisting the steers head. He throws him to the ground, amazing the entire stadium...

Announcer... "You saw it, but do you believe it? Time... Four point five two seconds, and let's give them a big hand for an outstanding performance."

As the stands explode in applause, Roamer trots back to Stoney, who mounts and rides over to shake hands with Hayes, who is sitting on Lotta Bucks grinning from ear to ear.

Shaking his hand, "You look like you're enjoying yourself."

"I am son, I surely am. But we got no time to sit out here yakkin about it; we still got more work to do."

Announcer, "Now don't go away because the funs just beginning, and our next event is truly the only two man event in rodeo.

Team Roping and it truly takes teamwork, with two ropers combining their roping and riding abilities. One roper, roping the steer's head while the other ropes his hind legs, and then they must position their horses in such a manner as to hold the steer between both horses. This is a timed event, with the shortest time being the winner. And our first contestants are Phil Davis out of Austin, Texas riding his horse Stormy, and Bob Evans out of Billings, Montana riding his horse Charlie Brown.

Sitting on their mounts, Stoney and Hayes watch the ropers back their horses to the back of the box and nervously wait for the chute to open. It does and their steer is off and running with the ropers close behind. Missing his first throw,

Phil hurriedly gathers his rope for another throw, which also misses.

Announcer, saying those two words no roper wants to hear, "No time.'

They watch three more entries, the last of which makes a time of six point nine seconds.

Announcer, "Our last contestants in this event will be Stoney Wood out of Oklahoma City riding his horse Roamer and our all time favorite cowboy Hayes Carlin out of Douglas, Arizona riding his horse Lotta Bucks."

As their slowly riding to the starting box, Stoney asks, "You want the head or heels?"

Laughing, "Boy, I thought you'd never ask. It's been a while since I threw a rope at one of these critters, so I better take the easy end, the one that sticks straight out there in front."

Smiling, "I kind of think you could take either end without much trouble."

Backing their horses to the back of the box, both men shake out their loops. Horses tensing, everyone is watching the chute. It opens, and the steer is off and running with Stoney and Hayes right behind it. Lotta Bucks is exactly where he's supposed to be, on the left side of the calf and about two steps in front of Roamer. Hayes makes his throw, catching the steer around its neck, turning the steer to the left, allowing Stoney to make his throw, catching both hind feet. As the steer falls, the two great horses separate, tightening their ropes just enough to keep the steer laying on its side. The judge drops his flag. Stoney and Hayes loosen their ropes, allowing the steer to stand and the ropes to fall off. The crowd is still cheering as Stoney is shaking hands with Hayes while they ride out of the arena.

Announcer, "Time… Five point two seconds. And I'd say these cowboys are having a pretty good day." Then, in his clear raspy voice, "Now hold on there a minute Hayes.

How about saying Hi to these good folks?" As Hayes waves his hat to the crowd, Stoney suddenly remembers why Hayes looked so familiar; he has been looking at his picture for years, hanging on his own bedroom wall.

The announcer continues. "And this is something you can tell your grandchildren about.

The day you saw Hayes Carlin, two-time National Grand Champion, All Around Cowboy. Let's give Hayes and his equally famous horse Lotta Bucks a big hand…. Hayes How about giving these good folks a wave?"

Stoney is grinning and shaking his head as applause explodes throughout the arena.. "I sure feel dumb. And to think I've got a picture of you hanging on my bedroom wall."

Smiling, "Well, it's probably an old picture."

"Yeah, well just wait until I tell everyone Hayes Carlin hazed for me."

Chuckling, "Yeah, well just wait until I tell everyone two time All American Stoney Wood, the guy who all the papers say just told the Dallas Cowboys to go pound sand, partnered with me in team roping."

Surprised, Stoney asks, "Is that what their saying?"

Nodding his head, 'That's about it."

"Well it's not really true, I just pulled my name out of the draft because I decided I didn't want to spend the rest of my life playing football."

Reining their horses in so they could talk, "I think you made a wise decision son, for whatever reason you made it.

Just remember you've always got friends out there, me included, friends you can call on anytime you need a little help from a friend."

Shaking hands, "Thanks Hayes and I'll never forget the day I met Hayes Carlin, a good man to call friend…"

"Ride tough son, an I'll probably be seeing you down the road somewhere, where I'd be more than happy to haze for you anytime. An if you ever get down around Arizona way, don't forget to stop in for a cup of coffee."

Nodding his head, "I'll sure do that."

They ride out of the arena side by side, where Stoney waits for the next event as he watches Hayes, still waving to his many fans, ride off behind the stands. He doesn't have long to wait.

Announcer, "And our next event of the afternoon will be calf roping, another timed event." In explanation, "When the calf leaves the chute, the cowboy races after him, setting off the timing clock when he crosses the barrier. He then must rope the calf, jump off his horse and throw the calf on his side. Then using a pigin string, he ties any three legs together, then throws his hands in the air. This Signals the timer to stop the clock. The calf must remain tied for six seconds before the time is official.

And, our first contestant will be Stoney Wood out of Oklahoma City riding Roamer, that big black and white stallion of his.

Shaking out a loop in his rope Stoney rides into the starting box as Roamer backs to the back of the box.

The great horse knows what's expected of him, tensing his muscles like a big spring, he's ready to explode out of the box the instant that calf leaves the chute. And suddenly the chute opens and Roamer is off and running after the calf.

Stoney swings his rope once, and lets it go. As his catch rope settles around the calf's neck, Stoney dallies his rope around his saddle horn and Roamer goes into a slide stop as Stoney, already halfway out of the saddle, is running down the rope as the calf hits the ground.

Roamer immediately slackens the rope, allowing the calf to stand just as Stoney gets to the calf.

Reaching across the calf, grabbing the calf's front leg with one hand and its flank with the other, he lifts the calf and drops it on its side.

Then taking the pigin string from between his teeth, he quickly wraps it around three of the calf's legs and secures it with a half hitch. Then throwing his hands in the air, he stands. The clock stops, the six second countdown begins...

Announcer, "Six point two seconds, and that folks could be hard to beat."

Stoney reaches down to loosen his throw rope, and removes his pigin string with a slight tug.

He mounts Roamer and coils his rope as he is leaving the arena to the sound of the crowd's applause. Then he turns to wait where he can watch the other contestants.

The next contestant has a time of seven point four two seconds. The next contestant misses his throw.

Cliff Walker, shaking out his loop riding Amigo, is about to enter the arena when one of the horses in front of Amigo kicks out, striking Amigo on his front right foreleg. Amigo jumps back, slightly limping. Both Stoney and Cliff are immediately off their horses.

Stoney examines Amigo's leg with his hands; "I don't think it's serious... Just sore... Better put some cold water on it to keep the swelling down."

Shaking his head in obvious disappointment, "I guess I won't be doing any roping today."

"What about your brother's horse?"

"He's not a rope horse."

Without hesitation, "Take Roamer."

Cliff looks at him like he might not have heard right. "Are you sure?"

"Go ahead, Roamer likes to chase calves. I'll put some cold water on Amigo's leg while you're gone."

Cliff mounts the great stallion and starts toward the arena then stops and turns. "Thanks."

Stoney just waves him off as he starts to lead Amigo over to a water hose.

Announcer, "Our next contestant is Cliff Walker out of Prescott, Arizona riding Amigo... No... Hold on there a minute... It looks like Walker will be riding Stoney Wood's big black and white stallion Roamer.

Cliff is a little nervous riding a new horse as he enters the box with Roamer. However, he relaxes almost immediately as the big horse, prancing with excitement, moves automatically to the rear of the box with his tail almost touching the rear wall.

As Cliff puts his pigin string in his mouth and shakes out his loop, he feels the tremendous energy flowing through Roamer. Almost in unison with the chute opening and the calf running as fast as it can out of the chute, Roamer's muscles un-coil and this great horse is on his way. Turning and dodging, the calf tries to get away... Roamer stays right with him, putting Cliff in position for his throw.

Cliff lets his rope fly, and as it's settling around the calf's neck and Roamer is going into his slide stop, Cliff is already out of the saddle and half way down the rope. Roamer slacks off on the rope, allowing the calf to stand just as Cliff reaches him, grabbing his foreleg and flank. He raises then lowers the calf to the ground and, with one knee on the calf, gathers three of his legs and wraps them with his pigin string, and throws his arms in the air. The flag drops and the crowd cheers.

Roamer walks over to Cliff, seemingly waiting with him for the six second count.

Announcer, "Time...Five point three six seconds... And let's give him a big hand for an outstanding performance... And our next contestant..."

Cliff gives Roamer a well-earned pat on the neck and then mounts. Shaking his rope loose he coils it and, giving a thrilled crowd, a wave rides out of the arena. Seeing Stoney over on the side putting water on Amigos leg, he rides over to him.

Cliff can't express enough praise for Roamer's performance. "I couldn't believe how fast Roamer came out of that box; it was almost like going from zero to sixty in about 2 seconds... He's quite a horse."

"Well from where I was standing, I'd say you did all right yourself. That was a great ride and a fantastic throw."

Not quite sure. "You're not upset?"

"Not a bit. Competition is what rodeos are all about. And the more competition we have, the better we have to become to compete, making it more interesting..."

Laughing, "Well I'm sure glad to hear you feel that way, because I plan on giving you a lot of competition in bronc riding. "

Smiling, "I guess we're just going to have to see about that."

Cliff and Stoney, leading Roamer and Amigo, are walking side by side toward the bucking chutes.

Cindy and Tim are on their feet, waiting for them as they approach the stands. Cindy doesn't appear to be the least surprised to see them walking together, just asking "What happened over there, you both got off your horses so fast and then you were both on the ground out of sight. *And seeming to forget it was really her argument.* I thought you guys were having another one of your stupid arguments, and I was just about to go over there, when I saw Cliff mount Roamer while you were holding Amigo."

They both laugh and Stoney explains. "Another horse kicked Amigo in his foreleg and he couldn't run on a sore leg, so I offered to let Cliff ride Roamer, so there's nothing to get all excited about."

"I'm not, as you say, all excited, I was just worried."

Holding his hand out to Cindy, Cliff offers his apologies. "I know I made a complete fool out of myself the other day, and I want you to know, I'm truly sorry for offending you."

Cindy smiles and shakes his hand. "Apologies accepted, and I want you to know I'm sorry for what I did to you, it could have hurt you very seriously."

Smiling, "Well it did kind of smart a little." They all burst into laughter.

"We have to get ready for some more bronc riding. Can you and Tim look after Roamer until I get back?"

Helping Tim onto Roamer's saddle, Cindy answers, "Of course, we can look after Amigo too if you like."

"Thanks for the offer, but I think I better pull his saddle and turn him out in one of those empty pens so he can walk around a little, so he won't stiffen up too much." Cliff says.

"Okay, but we'll still keep an eye on him."

As Cliff's leads Amigo to one of the empty stock pens, "She sure is a fiery little thing for being so pretty."

Stoney agrees, with a knowing smile. "She sure is that."

After pulling Amigo's saddle, they turn him out in a large empty pen where he has room to walk around. Then watch for a few minutes while he gets used to his surroundings, before going to the bucking chutes, where they help load some of the bronc's into the chutes as the announcer continues.

Announcer, "And you ain't seen nothing until you see this next event of ours... Bareback bronc riding, this will really make the hair on the back of your neck stand up. And our first contestant...."

Cliff and Stoney watch several contestants, but nothing too impressive. Jim comes over to join them and Cliff asks. "Where you been?" Then almost in the same breath, "Never mind, I can guess." And seeing puzzlement on Stoney face, nods to where a bunch of pretty cowgirls are sitting on the fence, and Stoney gives him a knowing smile.

As Stoney prepares to lower himself on his bronc.

The announcer is saying, "Our next contestant... Stoney Wood out of Oklahoma City, riding Black Jack, coming out of chute number three."

Stoney's bronc is in the chute and Cliff is advising him. "This one's a good horse, but he's notorious around here. He'll try to brush you off on the wall as soon as the gate opens, so watch him."

Stoney takes a deep seat then nods his head and the gate flies open with a bang. True to form, Black Jack tries to brush Stoney off on the wall before bolting for the opening with head down bucking as hard as he can, with Stoney helping him along, spurring every jump from chest to flanks.

With his head down, back bowed, twisting and turning, Black Jack bucks across the arena, the crowd is cheering as the eight-second buzzer sounds, and the pick up riders move in to pick Stoney off the bronc's back and release the flank strap.

Stoney swings off the pickup horse and, giving the cheering crowd a wave with his hat trots, back to the bucking chute.

As he reaches the chutes, the Announcer says, "Score... 75 and that makes Stoney Wood the man to beat."

Cliff pats him on the back and tells him. "Just don't get too confident, I haven't ridden yet."

"I wouldn't think of it, and I think you're up next so you better get ready. That is, if you can figure out which end of the horse to get on."

Announcer, "And our last contestant is Cliff Walker out of Prescott, Arizona riding Bold Storm, coming out of chute number two."

Stoney helps Cliff mount his bronc and just before the gate open, tells him, "Cowboy up!"

The gate flies open and Bold Storm comes out storming, head down back up, twisting and turning everyway but loose. With Cliff working his spurs all the way, Bold Storm is bucking his heart out and Cliff is sticking to him like glue, not a speck of daylight between the bronc and the seat of Cliff's pants, and the crowd loves it.

The eight second buzzer sounds. The pickup riders move in to pick Cliff up, Sliding off the pickup horse, Cliff walks back to the chutes while waving his hat.

Prejudice comes in all different colors and it is all wrong.

17

The Bulls

Announcer, "Score... 77, and give that cowboy a big hand
for an outstanding ride."

Jim and Stoney both jump off the chute to shake Cliff's
hand and pat him on the back.

"That was a great ride."

"I was just lucky; I got a great horse to ride. But let's not
be wasting time out here, cause this is when we separate the
men from the boys... Let's go ride some bulls."

The Announcer seems to agree with him. "Now this is
where we separate the men from the boys, Bull Riding.

And, keep in mind these bulls are wild animals, with a very
mean disposition, kinda like my mother in-law. They weigh as
much as two thousand pounds, and believe me when I tell you,
they don't want anyone even anywhere near them, much less
on their backs kicking them in their ribs. An to make matters
even worse they all seem capable of holding a grudge, and are
more than willing to inflict a little mayhem on any
unsuspecting young cowboy they happen to catch in their
sights.

And by that I mean, when they get one of these cowboys off
their backs, they're just as likely as not to turn on these
cowboys and try to do them as great a bodily harm as they

possibly can, and that's where the real heroes of rodeo, the bullfighters, come in.

Now I can understand how looking at them in their funny little clown outfits, they might look a little funny, but don't let that fool you, they're not really here for your amusement, they are here to protect these young cowboys. Believe me, these men are as courageous as they come.

Just ask any cowboy out here today, and he'll tell you he puts his life in the hands of these funny looking bullfighters every time he throws a leg over one of these bulls."

Stoney and Cliff are helping Jim get his bull rope around his bull, as Jim eases down on his bull, taking a deep seat. He wraps his bull rope around his hand and pulls the rope as tight as he can, just as the announcer says, "Now for our first contestant Jim Walker out of Prescott, Arizona, riding Awesome, coming out of chute number one."

Pulling his bull rope even tighter, Jim takes another wrap around his hand, tucking the loose end between his little finger (what is known as a suicide wrap) and gripping it in his tight fist, then nods his head. The gate slams open and Awesome comes out bucking, spinning, and twisting. Jim loses his seat almost immediately and begins to slide off the bulls back. Instead of letting go of his bull rope; he grips it even tighter and tries to pull himself back on the bull. When, with another buck and twist, Jim finds his hand is twisted under his bull rope and he's being dragged along the side of the bull. The bullfighters rush in, trying to free Jim's hand. Both men are thrown aside by the mad rushing bucks of the bull.

Stoney and Cliff both leap off the bucking chute.

Cliff runs along side the still wildly bucking bull, holding his brother up, trying to keep him on his feet so he doesn't get dragged under the bull where he'd surely get stomped to death.

Running on the other side of the bull, Stoney is trying to reach across the bull to release the bull rope.

The spectators are on their feet, more than a few women are screaming, seconds seem like hours.

Stoney is finally able to free Jims hand from the rope and the three of them fall, falling almost under the bulls kicking, thrashing feet.

The bull stops, and turning begins to lower his head and paw the earth, preparing to charge, when suddenly the two bullfighters run across in front of the bull distracting him.

One of them actually slaps the bull on his nose. The other bullfighter runs in front of the bull again, only this time, stopping to thumb his nose at the bull, while the other bull- fighter runs directly at the bull and to the cheers of the crowd, leaps over the bulls back, doing a magnificent job of distracting the bull.

Stoney and Cliff help Jim to his feet a little shaken, with Jim's cradling his right arm in his left. They hurry to the bucking chutes where several cowboys and one of the cowgirls are waiting to help Jim out of the arena and over to the first aid station.

Announcer, "Wheee... Now as soon as my blood pressure gets back to normal, we'll get on with a little more bull riding and our next contestant will be Stoney Wood out of..." Then noticing Stoney is still in the arena talking to Cliff, "Hey Stoney are you going to fool around out there all day, or are you going to ride some of these bulls?"

The crowd laughs as Stoney waves at the announcer and smiling, climbs back on the bucking chutes, where Cliff helps him get his bull rope on his bull. "I know this bull Stoney, and believe me, he's dangerous. He's a hooker like Bodacious was, and if he feels you leaning forward, he'll throw those horns at you so quick you won't see them coming. So watch him, or he'll plant one of those horns in your skull, and he'll spin to the right as soon as he clears the chute."

Announcer, "As I was saying, Stoney Wood out of Oklahoma City, riding Nightmare, out of chute number one."

Stoney takes a deep seat. Cliff asks "Ready?"

Stoney nods his head and the gate flies open.
Nightmare tries to live up to his name, as Stoney hears Cliff's belated, "And thanks."

Nightmare clears the chute and immediately spins to the right and throws his head back so fast, if he hadn't been warned, Nightmare may very well have caught him in the head with one of his horns.

Stoney has been working his spurs since the first jump out of the chute, and now even more determined, takes a firmer grip on his rope and concentrates on his bulls every move. Nightmare lowers his head even more and, twisting and turning, tries everything in his power to get rid of this thing on it's back. Turning and twisting and bucking all the way across the arena, with Stoney working his spurs all the way.

The crowd is on their feet cheering as the eight second buzzer sounds and a pickup rider comes in to take Stoney off his bull and sets him on the ground. As he's walking back to the bucking chutes. Announcer, Lets give that young man a big round of applause for an outstanding ride that earned him a score of... 76."

Cliff is waiting to congratulate him on his ride. "Well that wasn't too bad, in fact if you hang around me long enough, you might eventually learn how you're supposed to ride bulls."

They help a couple of other cowboys get on their bulls then Stoney says. "I think you're up next."

Announcer," And now for our last contestant of the day, Cliff Walker out of Prescott, Arizona, riding Twister, out of chute number three."

Cliff takes his seat and a firm grip on his rope, and nods his head.

The gate flies open, and Twister explodes out of the chute twisting to the left then twisting to the right. Cliff uses his spurs to make Twister start bucking with his head down, bucking all the way across the arena. The eight second buzzer sounds and the pickup rider picks Cliff up. Cliff slides off the pickup horse and is walking across the arena when the announcer says "And another good ride for this young man. His score 74... Let's give him a big hand.

Cliff is clearly disappointed, but smiles and waves his hat at the applauding spectators.

Stoney is waiting for him when he gets back to the bucking chutes, knowing the disappointment he's feeling. "It was still a great ride Cliff, you did everything right, it was just that your bull didn't have enough action."

"Thanks Stone, and I know your right. I felt it as soon as we came out of the chute."

"Yeah, I've been there and I expect I'll be there again. It's what we call, the luck of the draw."

"You got that right and I know we'll run into each other again somewhere down the road. When we do, I'll show how you're supposed to ride bulls."

"I'll count on it Cliff and I hope Jim will be all right."

"I'm sure he'll be alright He's tough and will probably ready to ride another bull in a day or two. Come on let's go by the office and see if we've got any money coming our way."

After leaving the office, Stoney goes over to where Cindy and Tim are waiting with Roamer, and hangs his bull rope, over the saddle horn. Sitting on Roamer Tim notices the bell. "That thing has a cow bell on it, is that to scare the bull?"

"No Tim, it's only on there for the weight. It helps the rope fall off the bull when the rider gets off."

Cindy says, "Yeah it sure didn't work for Jim and I'll have you know, that almost scared me to death. And then you and Cliff run out there like a couple of idiots, where you can get hurt too.'

"Jim needed our help, and there was no way we could just leave him out there."

"No, I suppose not, but it still scared me."

Nodding his head, "Yeah, it scared me too, but being scared is no excuse for not doing what you know has to be done."

Walking to the truck by Stoney's side with Tim riding Roamer, Cindy takes his hand. "I'll admit I was scared, in fact real scared, but I was also proud of you and yes, even Cliff for going out there to help Jim."

When they get to the truck, Stoney pulls the saddle off Roamer and gives him a good brushing and a long cool drink of water. Then opening the trailer, Roamer walks right in to a good serving of hay and oats.

Getting in the truck, Stoney removes a flat blue box from his shirt pocket and hands it to Tim.

Tim opens I, and excitedly shows it to his mother, a beautiful very large silver buckle, engraved with Champion all around cowboy and today's date. As he ruffles Tim's hair Stoney's tells him, "You're the Champion all around cowboy in this outfit, so I want you to have this."

Cindy's shaking her head. "You can't do this, it's too expensive."

"Why not"?

"Because it's… It's just too expensive."

"You already said that, but it will mean more to me knowing Tim has it."

Tim's exhausted, and it's only a matter of minutes until he's sound asleep with his head on his mother's lap while still clutching his new belt buckle.

"Do you want to stop for something to eat?"

"Thanks, but I think I better get Tim home where he can get some rest. I'll fix a little something for him to eat after he has a nice warm bath."

"Yeah, I guess we're all kind of worn out."

After a few minutes in a very quiet voice, "I was really kind of scared about going today, but I'm glad I did because it gave me a little insight into why Jim enjoyed rodeo so much, with all the color, excitement and the camaraderie between all the cowboys. I think any man would love it."

"You forgot one, challenge. The challenge of pitting yourself against others and against the animals."

"You make it sound like Roman gladiators entering the coliseum to test their strength and skills against others or knights in armor jousting in tournaments to find out who's the most worthy knight."

"Doesn't that sound like what we've been doing here today"?

"Yes, I suppose it does."
Stoney stops the truck out front and carries the still sleeping Tim into Cindy's little cabin and lays him on his bed.

"Thanks Stoney it really was a wonderful day."

"Thank you for coming."

We may use different words, but we all worship from our heart.

18

The Skinwalker Vision

After unloading Roamer and rubbing him down, Stoney starts his campfire. While cooking his dinner and drinking a cup of coffee, he thinks about today's events and his new friends, Hayes and Cliff. However, mostly about Tim, and trying to find the answer he has been looking so hard for.

Later that evening while gazing into the flames of his campfire, they increase and an image begins to appear... Four distinct mountains gradually appear as an image in the flames, which he associates with the four sacred mountains of the Navajo Nation. Suddenly two or three little black figures appear, and then almost immediately disappear in a grove of Cedar trees, only to reappear then once again disappear in the cedar trees.

The more he studies these little black figures, the more they appear to be trying to hide in the trees. The little black figures seem to be the answer he's been looking for, Skin Walkers. But what does it mean?

Laying in his bedroll that evening, gazing at the stars, Stoney tries to piece it all together, and when he wakes in the morning he still doesn't have all the answers. But, at least he believes he may know the cause, a Navajo Witch and his Skinwalkers.

Stoney has just gotten to the café, and is making the coffee when Lou arrives. Hurrying into his kitchen, he turns the grill on and puts a new apron on over his sparkling white tee shirt and white pants. Cindy and Darlene arrive a few minutes later, and are surprised to see Lou already there.

Cindy asks, "Will wonders never cease?"

"Now be nice ladies, he's just happy to see things are finally picking up around here." Then looking at Cindy, "And you especially should be happy"

"Now, just why do you think I should I be so happy this morning?"

"Because Lou just gave me the okay to hire some men from the reservation to clean the cabins up… including repairing the roofs."

"You're kidding... I could kiss him." Then, thinking about the thought of kissing Lou. "Well almost."

Laughing, "I've got a better idea… Let's get this place open before he changes his mind."

"Good idea." As she turns toward the front door, she stops and looks back at Stoney. "You said you'd only be here until the rodeo was over. So when are you leaving?"

"I thought I'd stick around for a little while, at least until I train the two new busboys Lou asked me to hire."

"Train? That shouldn't take more than ten minutes."

"Are you trying to degrade my profession, or are you just anxious to get rid of me?"

Laughing, "Neither, it was just that after you left last night, I suddenly realized I didn't know if I'd ever see you again."

"Well it kind of looks like you're going to have to put up with me for a little while longer. Now don't you think we should get this place opened?"

"Only if you promise to see that my roof gets fixed first just in case he really does change his mind."

Cindy and Darlene are busy waiting on tables, while Stoney is busy showing two young men, Billy and William from the reservation, the finer arts of bussing tables.
There are clean, white tablecloths on all the tables, the floors are clean and the little diner is busier than ever.

Later that morning, after introducing the two new bus boys to the waitresses, Stoney leaves the bussing of tables in the hands of his two protégés, while he directs two roofers and two carpenters from the Rez in the repairing of the cabins.

Cindy can't believe it, and has to come out of the busy diner to see for herself. "I can't believe this is actually happening, and Lou just told me you're even going to paint them."

"Both inside and out." Then trying to redirect their conversation, "I know Tim was pretty tired when we got home last night, how is he this morning?"

"Tired? He was exhausted, but after a good nights sleep he was his old self again."

"I haven't seen him this morning, is he home?"

"No, he's at Martha's; she usually looks after him while I'm working. Why?"

"I was just wondering, because I know how tired he was last night."

"Yeah, I really shouldn't have let him get that tired. But he had his heart set on going to the rodeo, and I never was very good at saying no to him."

"I know…" Then… "How long has Tim had leukemia?"

Giving him a questioning look. "Two years, maybe a little longer."

"Then it must have started shortly after his father's death?"

Getting upset with this line of questioning and the raising of memories, she had tried to put to rest. "Yes, but I don't really want to be standing out here talking about it."

Turning, Cindy starts to walk away, just as Stoney is saying, "I'm sorry Cindy, but it could be important."

Cindy looks over her shoulder, but continues walking back to the diner.

Stoney spends most of the day working on the cabins with the carpenters. On the few occasions he goes in the diner, Cindy appears to be avoiding him, even though she wanted so desperately to confront him, to ask what he meant when he said it could be important. However, thinking his questions about Tim and his father's death suddenly seemed to intrude too far into her own personal grief, she continued to avoid him.

Later that evening Cindy is looking out the window while washing dishes at the kitchen sink. Watching Stoney work around his campsite, while sparks from his campfire drift slowly into the night sky.

Picking up the phone, she calls Martha and asks if her daughter Alice could possibly come over to sit with Tim for a little while.

When Alice arrives, she throws a sweater over her shoulders and tells Tim she'll be right back.

Stoney is sitting by his fire having some coffee when Cindy walks into his camp, he stands and they look at each other for a moment before Cindy asks. "What did you mean?"

"About what?"

"You know perfectly well what I mean. About when you said it could be important."

Stoney looks at her for a minute with his deep penetrating eyes, then with a gentle but firm voice. "Sit down Cindy, let's talk."

She hesitates for just a moment then reaches for the folding camp chair.

"No, sit here by the fire where it's warm."

Handing her a cup of coffee. "To be honest, I really don't know if either my questions or your answers to them are important. But please believe me when I tell you, I wasn't asking them just to be prying into your personal life.

I was only asked because I believe there could possibly, and I said possibly, be more to this than we imagine."

"I don't understand what you mean."

"No, I don't imagine you do, as most people wouldn't. However do me a favor, just sit back, relax, and gaze into the fire." She does what he says. "That's it, just relax. I'm going to ask you a few questions and I want you to answer as truthfully as you can, and don't be surprised at anything you may see or think you see in the fire…

Now you told me earlier that Tim's illness began shortly after his father's death. Can you be a little more specific as to how soon after his death?"

Sounding almost, as if, she was in a trance. "Five… Five or six.. Maybe six months after Jim's death, at least as far as the doctors have been able to determine. I remember thinking how could this possibly be happening to us, so soon after his father's death?"

"I know from what you've told me Tim was very young when his father passed away, but were they very close?"

Sounding upbeat, almost happy, "Oh yes, Jim lived for his son and they were together constantly when Jim was home. Tim could hardly wait for his father to get home from work, and if he was late coming home, or if Jim had to work late, or had to work on weekends, Timmy would get upset. But when his father would finally get home, Timmy would be all smiles… Jim would play with Timmy on the floor or read to him, or let him help in the garden, or let him help wash the car." Tears come to her eyes, as she looks into the fire, "Ohhhhh I can see him … I can see him, he's smiling… He looks sooo happy."

"Yes, I know and he is happy, he's happy for both you and Timmy… Now… Did Jim ever talk to you about traditional Navajo heritage or beliefs?"

"We talked about everything. He told me how happy he had been as a child growing up on the reservation... The Rez as he used to call it."

"Did he ever say anything to you about Navajo healers or medicine men?"

"I remember one time, he told me about what he called Bad Medicine... something about the Navajo Witches and their Skinwalkers. But when I told him it was just superstition, he wouldn't talk about it anymore."

"What did he tell you about the Skinwalkers?"

"He said they roamed around in skins of animals, casting spells and doing all kinds of bad things for the witches.

He said they could change from a human form to animal form in just a snap of your fingers... When I told him it was all superstitious nonsense, or maybe there were some men who really did wear animal skins to scare people but they couldn't change into animals, he got upset with me." Pausing then, "I remember he told me he once had a friend whose father was a Witch."

"He said he once had a friend whose father was a witch. Did he tell you what happened to this friend or why they weren't still friends?"

"No. I think he was upset with me for not taking him serious."

"All right Cindy, that's all the questions for now, and you will remember our conversation fully when speaking only to me in private. However, around anyone else, you will remember it only as a dream. Now let me freshen your coffee."

Cindy gives him her cold cup of coffee, which he sets aside and hands her a cup of hot coffee.

"Did... Did what I think happen, really happen?"

Stoney only nods his head.

"Oh, my god... Was I hypnotized?"

"In a sense, but actually your mind was only enhanced so you would clearly remember some of the things you and Jim spoke of."

"You mean things like Navajo Witches and Skinwalkers? When Stoney nods, Cindy continues, "Well I want you to know, I don't believe in witchcraft."

"Tell me why is it that most everyone believes the Australian Aborigines have supernatural powers, yet are unwilling to accept the fact certain Native American Indians have these same powers?"

"Is it truly fact?"

Once again Stoney only nods.

"Jim once told me he actually saw spirits and I laughed at him."

"You should not have laughed at him."

"Are you telling me you've seen spirits?"

"Did you not see Jim's image in the flames of this fire?"

Looking at the fire and sounding shocked with the realization of what she had seen "Oh my god, I did." Then... "What does it mean?"

"Truthfully, I don't know because at this time I only have a very slight suspicion. But first I should probably explain.

Both Jim and Timmy are Navajo, and don't tell me Timmy is only half Navajo. There is no such thing as half Navajo or half Sioux or half Apache or half Cherokee.

Tim is Navajo, and the Navajo believe everything is intertwined, everything from the smallest leaf to the largest, darkest thundercloud. They believe everyone must live in harmony, harmony with the earth, as well as with each other and most importantly, in harmony within oneself.

This harmony in their lives extends even to their speech, which to a Navajo is sacred, and even to speak disrespectful to another person violates their harmony.

They believe if harmony is disrupted or is not maintained for any reason within oneself, it could result in illness or even tragedy.

Now you tell me that, even as young as Tim was, he and his father were very devoted to each other. And what I'm saying is the loss of his father would have undoubtedly disrupted his harmony."

Shaking her head, seemingly in disbelief, "I don't know if I should laugh or cry... Because I truly don't know what to believe."

"Cry if you must, but don't laugh at what you do not understand."

"But what about these... these Navajo Witches and Skinwalkers?"

Not wanting to upset her any more than he already has, he tries to evade her question. "We're not talking about witches or skinwalkers, as at this time I don't know they are actually involved."

"But you're saying they actually exist?"

Realizing he is not going to be able to evade her question, "Yes, they do exist, but I think I should explain. A Navajo Witch is not like the old fictional SalemWitch you've read about, he is a Navajo healer who is using his powers for other things besides healing, what Navajos call bad medicine. While a Navajo Witch does have powers, his powers are not nearly as strong as a healer who devotes his entire life making good medicine.

Yet the power of bad medicine a witch possesses is strong, and they sometimes use this power against others who may have offended them or on behalf of someone else who has been offended, someone who may go to a witch seeking vengeance against whoever they feel has offended them. Because a witch's power is more effective when a person's harmony is in conflict with their inner being, the witch may send his Skinwalkers out to watch his intended victims to learn when their harmony is in discord, in order to learn when their powers may best be used." Pausing for a moment, then continuing. "However as I said, we have no reason to believe this is what happened here. While Jim may very well have offended someone from the reservation, Timmy was far too young to have done so."

Still finding it difficult to believe they are even talking about witches and skinwalkers, Cindy asks, "But could it have been because Jim was no longer here they took their vengeances against Timmy?"

Stoney answers hesitantly, because he has had these same thoughts, "Yes that is possible. However, we don't know that is what actually happened."

"If the doctors were unable to help Timmy, how could a healer help?"

"I don't really know they can, but becoming a healer is not like going to a university for eight years or so.

A Navajo healer spends sixteen, seventeen, or even eighteen years learning herbs, the powders and elixirs made from them, and literally hundreds of healing chants and dances, with each word and each step in its precise place.

These are not formulas that have been written down in books, but sets of specific instructions that have been passed down from one healer to another for thousands of years.

And naturally you are asking yourself, does it really work?

The Navajo's also have very modern and up-to-date state of the art medical facilities throughout the reservation with some of the finest, brightest medical doctors in the country, and these highly trained medical doctors do not hesitate to work hand in hand with Navajo healers because they know it works.

Some of these brilliant surgeons have even elected to use healers in the curing of their own ills, as well as the ills of their own children."

"I guess I still don't understand, are you asking me to believe Timmy's problem was caused by a Witch or from the shock of his father's death?"

"No, because I'm not sure that is actually what happened. I'm only telling you of the possibility and only that because Timmy is Navajo. I'm asking you to keep an entirely open mind, even to things you do not fully understand."

"But to even imagine such an illness as leukemia could possibly be caused by some Skinwalkers or because his harmony was thrown out of whack by his fathers death seems ridiculous."

"Were the doctors able to tell you the cause of his leukemia?"

"No, in fact they were very evasive." Falling silent for a minute then, Cindy asks, "If it's possible for a Navajo Healer to heal Timmy, why don't we take him to a healer tonight?"

Hesitating, because he knows this is not the answer she wants to hear, "Because it is not yet time."

"When will it be time?"

"We will know when it is time."

With tears streaming down her cheeks, "Oh god Stoney, I feel so alone."

"You're not alone, as you saw this evening Jim will always be with you..."

Smiling through her tears. "Yes, as he came to me tonight."

"Now you don't want Timmy to see those tears, so dry your eyes and I'll walk you home."

Nodding, "All right but first I think I need another cup of coffee."

Stoney pours them both a cup of coffee and while they're sipping their coffee.

"Tell me Stoney, who are you? And don't tell me you're just a cowboy going down the road. There's more to you than that. I feel it whenever I'm with you, I feel a calmness and gentleness around you, and if anyone else had told me just half of what you told me tonight, I'd tell them they were nuts.

Yet as crazy as everything you have told me sounds, I find I actually tend to believe you, or at least believe in you.
You've told me on several occasions to have faith, and it may sound funny, but just being with you seems to give me faith."

"I also told you once that I was a wanderer and that pretty much says it all. As for faith, faith is really all any of us have."

After walking Cindy home, Stoney returns to his camp where he stretches out in his bedroll, only sleep doesn't come, all he can think about is this terminally ill little kid.

He knows the Great Spirit has placed him here to help this child, but is at a complete loss as to what he can do.
Getting out of his bedroll, Stoney rekindles the fire. And, gazing into its flames begins to chant. The flames soon brighten and Black Eagle's image appears in the flames.

Stoney passes his thoughts to his grandfather, explaining about the child and his suspicion that a Navajo Witch and his Skinwalkers may be involved in the child's illness. Hesitantly he admits he doesn't know if even the mighty powers of the White Buffalo are powerful enough to cure a terminally ill child with leukemia.

Black Eagle explains that if this child is to be healed, the healing will not come from White Buffalo, but from the Great Spirit. Then he cautions his grandson to have patience, and when the time is right the Great Spirit will show him the way.

The image of black Eagle fades, but Stoney continues to sit by the fire gazing into its flames while thinking about what his grandfather has told him, until there are only warm embers remaining in his campfire.

Stoney is repairing a window shutter on one of the cabins when Sally and Cindy bring some donuts and coffee over for the workers. For reasons unknown, Sally cannot seem to stop laughing. And of course Stoney has to ask. "What's going on?"

A little embarrassed Cindy answers, "Don't pay any attention to her; she thinks everything's funny."

Hearing this, Sally bursts out laughing again.

"Come on; tell me what's so funny?"

"Sally, you better not tell him."

Even without knowing what Sally's laughing about, Stoney's starting to laugh himself.

"All right, all right. I'll tell you, but it's not really all that funny and besides it's all your fault.'

"My fault, what did I do?"

"It's not what you did, it's what you didn't do."

Throwing his hands in the air, "All right I give up, what didn't I do?"

"When you introduced the new buss boys to us, you just said, this is Billy and this is William."

"What's wrong with that?"

"Well you at least could have told us their last names."

"I guess I'm a little dense this morning, because I still don't understand."

"All I did was ask Billy what his last name was and he said Billy, so I asked him again what his last name was and he said Billy. Well, I just knew he could not have possibly understood me so I said no, I mean your last name, and he looked me straight in the eye and said Billy.

I must have stood there for at least three minutes asking him what his last name was. Everyone was standing around laughing and I was getting upset because I thought they were laughing at Billy... But they weren't really laughing at Billy; they were laughing at me, but I didn't know that at the time. Because everyone except me knew, his name was Billy Billy. And that wasn't bad enough, to make matters worse, I turned to William and asked him what his last name was and do you know what he said?"

"Yeah, he said Billy. They are brothers, so naturally they have the same last name. But to clear matters up, you should have asked them what their middle name was."

"No way, they probably would have said Billy."

"No, they would have said Samuel, Billy Samuel Billy and William Samuel Billy.'

"You're kidding."

And with a straight face "Fraid not."

"Smart aleck! Just see if I bring you any more donuts."

Mid afternoon in the little diner, business has let up for a few minutes, and Cindy, Sally and Darlene are relaxing with a coke.

Darlene is complaining about her feet. "Boy I've got to do something about that corn on my toe."

Setting her coke on the counter Sally says. "If business keeps up this way we're all going to have corns."

"Well don't knock it. At least we're starting to make some money. I've even been able to pay my child care."

"Yes it definitely has its advantages, but my feet still hurt."

"How's Tim doing?"

"Pretty good, they did some more tests the other day and he's due for another checkup. Stoney's going to drive us to the hospital this evening."

Cindy and Stoney are watching as the Doctor is finishing Tim's examination.

As nurse Julie helps him on with his shirt. "Now how about you coming into the other room with me so I can show you the pictures of my new kitten?

And as Tim steps out of the room with the nurse, the doctor nods toward the closing door, "He seems to be holding up very well. Considering out latest tests indicate a definite increase in his white cell count."

Stoney asks. "Is there any chance of it reversing its self?"

Slowly shaking his head, the Doctor hesitantly replies, "At this stage, our only hope seems to be for a transplant."

Cindy's eyes are misting "And we can't have a transplant without a match."

The Doctor is slowly shaking his head. "Believe me; we're doing everything we can. Knowing Timmy is part Navajo, we've even contacted the National Health Service on the reservation and while they've had many volunteers, we still don't have a match."

Looking at Cindy, Stoney inquires of the Doctor. "How long do we have to find a match?"

"As I told Mrs. Morris, only as long as he's strong enough to undergo a transplant operation. And with our tests indicating a definite acceleration in the increase of white blood cells, it's hard to say. Maybe a month or it may be only a matter of a few weeks, or even days."

Wiping her eyes and with difficulty even speaking "Aaa... And when that happens, is there anything else we can do?"

Removing his glasses and looking down at his desk. "As I've told you, when it reaches that stage there's not much anyone can do except make him as comfortable as possible."

Cindy is looking like she is about to collapse. Stoney helps her to a chair and the Doctor pours a glass of water for her, and then asks "Would you like me to prescribe something for you?"

Shaking her head no, "Just give me a few minutes and I'll be all right."

Cindy and Stoney are both quiet on the drive home, engrossed in their own thoughts. Timmy on the other hand can't seem to stop talking about the new puppies at Martha's house.

When they arrive at Cindy's newly painted cabin Stoney asks. "Do you want me to come in for a little while?"

"No, I think I want to be alone for a little while."

"All right, but if there's anything I can do just holler."

After starting his campfire, he picks up a brush, and walking over to Roamer begins to brush him while thinking about what the Doctor said, which was pretty much, what they have suspected.

Knowing they are running out of time Stoney goes back to his campfire where he sits for hours, chanting as Black Eagle has taught him, praying for some kind of sign.

Suddenly the flames in his little campfire become much brighter and, gazing into these flames, he sees a vision of a Navajo Hogan then its doorway. As if he were entering the Hogan, first he sees a small purification fire made from the wood of four different trees, then a large medicine sand painting. The sand painting representing the ancient tale *Reared within the Mountains,* with Timmy's little form lying in the center of the sand painting.

The vision slowly fades only to reappears as the *"Hunters Dance"* with the dancers chanting and waving an arrow in their hands as they dance around a figure dressed in white, holding a child wrapped in a white blanket extended in his arms. Moving closer and closer, the dancers begin touching the child with their arrows. Touching the child's back then his chest and his head, touching every part of his body, driving the evil spirits from this child's body.

Once again, the vision in the fire slowly fades only to brighten moments later, showing The *Fire Dance* with its many dancers, dancing around a large ceremonial fire, each dancer following close in line of the dancer in front. The dancers, wearing only ceremonial paint and waving wands of flaming eagle down, are often striking the bare backs of the dancer in front, then striking their own bare backs, with their burning wands. While in the background, hundreds of Navajos men women and children lend their many voices and prayers to the sing, magnifying the power of the most sacred of all Navajo healing chants, *The Mountain Chant.*

Little black figures continue to appear as if peeking out from behind the trees, only to disappear again, the Skinwalkers. The fire suddenly brightens and another sand painting appears. The painting depicts Jim Light Horse Morris and his son Timmy, done with black and light gray sand. A figure appears, a small man with small beady eyes, long gray scraggly hair, and a jagged scar on his right cheek. Two shadowy figures can be seen over his shoulder, then slowly the vision fades.

Stoney sits by the fire, long after there is nothing left in the fire except warm ash.

Thinking about what he has seen and what he has been asked to do, only hoping he will be able to accomplish his task in time.

Authors note: Please do not disregard Skinwalkers as fantasy. While this author has never had an encounter with a Skinwalker, many Navajos through the years have experienced uncountable encounters with Skinwalkers, as evidenced by one such encounter told to me by my dear friend, Billy Samuel Billy.
If you were to ask me if I believed him, I would answer, absolutely.

19

Evening Star

Stoney is up at the crack of dawn, ready to start his run when he hears the screeching of an eagle, Looking up into an almost cloudless blue sky, he sees an eagle circling high above. As he begins his run, he notices the eagle continues to circle above, as if telling him, he is not alone and the time is near.

Later that morning as he is working on the cabins, he hears the screech of the eagle and, looking up, sees the eagle is still with him, telling him his hour of need is near.

When the workers stop for lunch, Stoney goes into the diner and helps himself to a glass of water, and finds a seat at the end of the counter. Sally asks what he would like for lunch. After placing his order, he watches Cindy as she waits on some customers. Looking lethargic, it's obvious Cindy didn't get much rest. After placing an order with Lou, Cindy stops near where Stoney is sitting to pick up silverware and napkins. Feeling Stoney's gaze, she turns and smiles "Yeah, don't say it, I didn't get any rest, I just tossed and turned and couldn't get to sleep."

"I didn't do much better myself." Then, "How's Timmy this morning?"

"He looks better than we do. I thought about keeping him home this morning. But decided it was better to let him go to Martha's like he always does."

"That was probably best." Stoney says in agreement.

Nodding her head she goes back to work, and Stoney half-heartily begins to eat his lunch. He is about half through with his lunch when the phone behind the counter rings and, before Sally answers it, Stoney knows.

Sally turns and calls to Cindy who starts to walk to the phone, then suddenly runs, picking up the phone, and listens. Dropping the phone, Cindy sags, bracing herself on the rear counter, turns to Sally and Stoney, "He's... He's collapsed."

Taking Cindy by the arm, Stoney tells Sally. "I'll take her."

With her hand to her mouth, "Oh my god... Call me if there's anything I can do."

Rushing out of the diner and opening the door to his truck... "Get in, we'll take my truck."

Unnoticed by either of them, the eagle is soaring in the hot rising thermals above the café. Racing down the three lane highway, it doesn't take them long to get to Martha's, who holds the door open for them as they rush in. Timmy is lying on the floor among some scattered toys; Cindy screams and rushes to her son. Stoney kneels beside Timmy, feeling for his pulse and checking his breathing. Martha's crying.

Stoney picks Timmy up off the floor and as he's carrying him toward the door "Let's go."

Not knowing what else to do, Cindy rushes ahead and opens the screen door. Then at the truck, Stoney tells her to get in the truck. She does and Stoney places Timmy in her lap then gets in the truck himself. With tires spinning in the loose gravel, he races out the driveway onto the highway, heading toward Riverton.

It takes Cindy several minutes to realize where they are. "We should have called the hospital to tell them we were coming."

Stoney's shaking his head, "We aren't going to the hospital."

Looking shocked, Cindy asks, "Not going to the hospital? We have to go to the hospital."

"No, they already told us they couldn't do any more for Timmy."

"Then where are we going?"

"To the reservation."

Cindy slowly shakes her head, as tears swell in her eyes, "Oh my god."

"Trust me Cindy, the reservation is our only hope."

Tears are streaming down her face as Stoney turns into the reservation. Seeing several men talking in a parking lot, he swings the truck into the parking lot. Jumping out, he asks them where the Council office is.

One of the men points to an office building, at the far end of the parking lot. Thanking them, he hurriedly gets back in the truck and drives over to the office building. As he does, he notices the eagle soaring above the office building.

Leaving Cindy and Tim in the truck, he hurries into the building. Where, he finds a receptionist working on her computer.

Looking up, "May I help you?"

"Yes, I have to speak to the Council person."

"Do you have an appointment?"

Another woman comes out of a side door and seemingly ignoring Stoney, begins looking through a file cabinet.

"No I don't, but this is an emergency and it can't wait, I must speak to the Council person right away."

"I'm sorry sir bu…" The receptionist, is suddenly interrupted, by the woman at the file cabinet. Who has heard the urgency in Stoney's voice, "I'm Council Delegate Evening Star, What's so important it can't wait?"

"I have a sick child outside that needs our help."

"What do you want me to do, call for medical assistance?"

""No, the doctors have already done everything they can. I want your best drummers, dancers and two of your most powerful healers. I want a healing ceremony. I want a Mountain Chant healing ceremony."

"And you are?"

"Stoney Wood, of the Rainbolt."

"And Black Eagle?"

"My Grandfather."

"You're aware the Mountain Chant ceremony usually requires nine days."

"We don't have nine days, we may not even have nine hours."

"What's wrong with this child?"

"Leukemia."

"His name?"

"Tim Morris, son of Jim Light Horse Morris."

"Where's his father?

"He was killed three years ago in a rodeo accident."

"And his mother?"

"Outside in my truck."

The Delegate looks Stoney in the eye... Then, as she turns away. "Wait here." and she steps out of the room

Stoney anxiously awaits the Delegates return, and suddenly the door opens and four men dressed in suits hurry out, only giving Stoney a quick glance as they leave the building. Watching them leave, Stoney isn't aware of the Delegates return until "You will have your healing ceremony. Now take me to my grandson."

Hardly believing the turn of events, Stoney hurriedly opens the door and shows Evening Star to his truck and opens the passenger door.

"Cindy, this is your mother in-law, Tim's grandmother Evening Star Morris. And Evening Star, this is your daughter in-law Cindy Morris and your grandson Tim."

Kneeling by the open door, Evening Star reprimands Stoney. "You should know better, this is my Daughter and Grandson." She gently lays her hand, on Tim's cheek then firmly grasping Cindy's hand in hers, have faith... We must have faith…. Now we're going home."

Stoney says, "We'll follow you."

Giving Stoney the keys to her car, "No, you'll follow us, I'll drive my daughter and grandson home."

As Stoney's following Evening Star, who's driving his truck, he's thinking this is really some kind of lady."

Evening Star soon turns into the driveway of a small, neatly landscaped house. Stoney pulls in behind them and hurrying to the truck opens the passenger door and asks. "May I carry Timmy?"

"Of course you may, just be careful." Then hurrying to open the front door and indicating a bedroom. "Just take him in there. That was Jim's room, and now it is my daughters' room."

Cindy follows Stoney into the bedroom, and watches as he gently lays Tim on the bed.

Evening Star takes Cindy's hand and guides her to the bed. "Why don't you lay beside him and rest? For what we must do, you will need all the rest you can get." Then indicating Stoney, "Just leave everything to this young man and myself. Now relax, and I'll bring you a cup of tea in a few minutes." And laying a light blanket over Cindy and Tim, Evening Star and Stoney leave the room.

Looking around the room, Cindy sees pictures of Jim as a child and one as a teenager standing by a man who she decides must have been his father, and several trophies on the dresser. But what she doesn't see is dust…

There isn't a speck of dust anywhere in the room and tears come to her eyes as she pictures this nice little lady taking care of this her sons room, in the hope that someday he will return.

She suddenly feels completely relaxed, knowing no harm will come to either Tim or her in this home.

Evening Star is telling Stoney. "I gave instructions to close the reservation to all tourists. As the Mountain Chant is for no eyes or ears but ours.

The drums will begin soon, summoning all who can come.

The Tribal police will allow only Navajo near the sacred circle. Dancers and Healers have been notified their presence has been requested" As she is speaking the drums begin…

"Good, the drums are calling the tribe together. There will be talking drums on every mountaintop, telling our people of our need of their voices and prayers for our sing.

Those who are unable to reach us because of distance will gather wherever they can across our Nation to offer us their voice and prayers.

As you know, the holy men are not allowed to begin the Sand Painting you requested until sunset, but it will be ready for a night healing.

"Now tell me how you intend to perform The Mountain Chant, a nine day ceremony, in hours?"

Shaking his head, "I know how ridiculous it must seem. But I can only tell you that I have been instructed to do so, and I can only hope your Healers will understand for I need their help."

"Your Grandfather's powers are well known and respected by every tribe and medicine man in the country. Our Healers will not only understand, they will do as you request."

"Thank you, now if I may trouble you for the use of a Hogan, preferably near the sacred circle.'

"Of course, I'll ask someone to show you the way. But first, tell me, are Skinwalkers involved with my grandson's illness?"

"I suspect they are, and while I don't know the name of the man involved, I can tell you he's a small man with gray hair and a long jagged scar on his right cheek."

Nodding her head, "The man you described is Willie Pale Deer McGaw. His son Paul and Jim were very close friends until Paul was killed in an automobile accident. His father Willie had been drinking, and was driving the car when the accident occurred. That's how he got the scar. Paul was in the front seat and Jim was in the back seat when Willie ran off the road and hit a tree. Paul wasn't wearing his seat belt and was thrown through the windshield, killing him instantly. Jim was unhurt, but it took several months before he got over the shock of his friend's death. Willie needed someone to blame for his son's death besides himself, so he blamed his son's death on Jim, saying Jim should have died instead of Paul." Shaking her head, "Jim started drinking after Paul was killed and we had several arguments about his drinking, and I believe those arguments were the reason Jim left home."

"That may be why he left home, but I know for a fact Jim didn't drink. When I knew him, he wouldn't touch a drop. It was well known that Jim would take his younger classmates aside and tell them how alcohol was our worst enemy." Nodding, "Now I know why he felt so strong about not using alcohol."

"Thanks Stoney, you don't know how I've worried these last few years, not knowing what Jim was doing, so it's good to hear he was doing good."

"I didn't know Jim very well, but everything I've heard about him was good, and you only have to look in the other room to find two people who loved him with all their hearts." Pausing then, "Jim once mentioned to Cindy that he used to have a friend whose father was a Witch. Do you know if he was referring to Willie Pale Deer?"

Nodding, "Yes it is said Pale Deer is a Witch."

"Does he still live on the reservation?"

"I haven't heard anything about him in several years, but he used to live in an old trailer about eight miles up the old Mine road, and I understand he has every herb, potion and spell he's concocted over the last forty years in that old raggedy trailer. But if you're thinking about going to see Pale Deer, I wouldn't, Pale Deer is said to be a very powerful Witch."

"I feel Pale Deer needs to learn a lesson, but I have no intention of going there myself. Now I think I should go to the

Hogan to meet with your healers and I want to thank you again for understanding. I'll return for Tim before sunset."

"Then if you will pardon me, I would like to serve my daughter some tea."

20

Talking Drums

Stoney is shown to a small Hogan by his guide, one of several only a few steps from the sacred circle. Upon entering, he is pleased to see someone has already started a fire. The floor of the Hogan is covered with beautiful brightly colored hand woven rugs.

Removing his boots, he slips his moccasins on, and places the package he has taken from his truck on the earthen shelf encircling the interior of the Hogan. He sits by the fire and, while gazing into its flames, thinks of his grandfather.

Black Eagle's image soon appears in the flames, and they exchange their thoughts.

Within minutes, the talking drums at Black Eagle Valley begin, and soon drums of every tribe in the country will be telling of the healing ceremony of a child, calling the people together. In minutes, dancers will begin dancing their prayers; medicine men will begin chanting, all for the healing of a child. A child they know nothing of, only that it's a child who needs their prayers.

By the time the first dancers and healers arrive, Stoney has changed into his deerskin breeches, shirt, and moccasins and is wearing a white headband and his eagle feather.

Inviting them into his Hogan and asking them to be seated around the fire, he offers them a smoke from his sacred pipe, while he explains in their own tongue what he needs.
The healers show Stoney the Hogan they will use for the healing sand painting.
Assistants begin cleaning the Hogan. Holy men begin purifying both inside and outside of the Hogan. Assistants gather four kinds of wood for the sacred fire. They gather coal and corn pollen for fragrance.

As Evening Star said, the talking drums are sounding on every mountaintop throughout the Nation.

Navajo families everywhere within sound of these drums begin gathering their families together, carrying blankets and something to eat, answer the call to the sacred circle.

They come singly, in twos and threes, and they come in droves, many walking, some riding horses or mules, or driving old cars or old trucks, or driving horse drawn wagons picking up neighbors and friends. Helping each other as is Navajo tradition.

Navajos come by the hundreds, with more coming all the time. They gather around the sacred circle, waiting for sunset.

The tribal police have closed this immediate area of the reservation to all but Navajo.

Evening Star has been visiting with her daughter, learning as much as she can of this beautiful young lady she has taken to her heart as her true daughter.

"We should begin preparing for the ceremony soon, but first let me bring you a cup of soup, for you will need all the energy you possess."

Evening Star brings Cindy some soup, and when she finishes she takes the dishes away, then returns with a beautiful ankle length soft deerskin dress and knee high moccasins, both trimmed with brightly colored beads, handing them to Cindy.

"We should get ready for the healing."

As she slips into the deerskin dress, Cindy asks, "What's the healing?"

"A healing is when the tribe, medicine men, and holy men come together to dance and sing their prayers to the Supreme Being , asking him for a healing of a loved one."

Looking at Tim, "Will it make him better?" Cindy asks.

"I know it's particularly, difficult for someone not raised in our ways to understand and believe as we do… I learned just this afternoon that I lost a son… Then I also learned that I was given a Grandson and a Daughter. I do not want to ever lose either of you. So yes, I believe as you must believe."

Tears glistening in her eyes... "Oh, I want so much to believe as you do."

"Then do." And stepping over to Cindy, she puts her arms around her.

While looking at herself in the mirror, Cindy remarks "It's beautiful."

"Yes it is… But it needs… Just a moment, I'll be right back. When evening Star returns she has a beautiful matching silver and turquoise belt and necklace and a beautiful hand woven Navajo shawl which she drapes over Cindy's shoulders. Then Evening Star steps back to look at Cindy wearing the turquoise necklace and belt. "Turquoise stones, besides being very beautiful, are also very sacred to the Navajo. On you, they look exceptionally beautiful."

"Now just relax and rest here with Tim while I get dressed and then I would like to talk to you before Stoney arrives."

21

Gathering of Nations

While at the Rainbolt ranch, John has just gotten home from the office and is walking into the kitchen. Setting his briefcase on the counter asks, "What in the world are all those drums?"

As Peggy pours him a glass of iced tea, "I don't really know, but they started about an hour ago."

"Black Eagle has ceremonies all the time, but I can't ever remember hearing the drums and the sound of these drums seem to be resonating right out of the ground."

"Yes, it does sound like a mother drum and they do say a mother drum actually does resonate through our mother earth."

As Peggy and john are having their dinner, one of the house keepers enter, Caroline, Native American, forties, and says, "Pardon me for disturbing you during dinner."

"That's perfectly all right Caroline, what can we do for you?" Peggy asks.

"Dorothy and I would like to know if you will be needing us this evening."

"I don't believe so Caroline, why do you ask?"

"We would like to go to Black Eagle's camp."

"Of course you may go."

Setting his napkin down, John asks, "Do you know what the drums are saying?"

'They are calling the people together for a medicine dance."

"Do you know who the medicine dance is for?"

"No, the drums do not yet say."

"Is Black Eagle all right?"

"Yes, the dance is not for Black Eagle."

"Thank you Caroline. And of course you and Dorothy may go, and be sure to tell Black Eagle we asked about him."

"I will sir, but you should also come."

"Thank you, but I have some reports I must go over this evening."

Caroline thanks them again, then turns and goes out the door.

Watching Caroline leave, Peggy suggests. "Maybe we should go."

"I can't honey, these reports are important and I must go over them."

Evening star returns and finds Cindy standing at the dresser crying, while holding a picture of Jim in her hand. Understanding her anguish, Evening Star puts her arms around Cindy...

"I know you loved each other very much and we will have many evenings to talk about it. However, now we must be brave and only think about this evening and his son, who will carry his father's name and will, from this evening on, be known as Tim Light Horse Morris ...

As I am known as Evening Star and from this moment on you will be known as Morning Star... The brightest star of all.... Now we must talk... As I said, I know it is very difficult for someone not raised in our ways to believe as we believe.

I also know you will be both seeing and hearing many strange things this evening, strange to your eyes, things you will neither understand nor believe even after seeing them.

However, what you will be seeing is very sacred to us, and I ask you not to cry out or show even the slightest sign of either shock or disbelief... Above all else, what you see must remain here for it is only for Navajo, and from this evening on you are Navajo for you are my daughter.

There's a knock on the door. "That must be Stoney, I'll let him in."

Evening Star opens the door for Stoney who's carrying a package wrapped in plain brown paper and tied with heavy white cord. Seeing Evening Star is ready he says, "If you'll allow me just a few minutes to change we'll be ready to go."

Evening Star directs him to a room and, while Stoney is changing, Evening Star and Cindy wrap Tim in a warm white Navajo blanket.

Stoney returns, wearing his White Buffalo ceremonial regalia, pure white deerskin shirt, decorated with lacings and fringe across the back of his shoulders and sleeves, pure white breeches and moccasins, and with his eagle feather hanging from a white band around his forehead. As he steps into the room, Evening Star says. "I understand you've requested two dances, the Fire dance and the Hunters dance.

Nodding his head, Stoney answers, "As I was instructed."

Understanding, Evening Star says, "The Hunters dance is done to combat evil spells cast by Witches and Skinwalkers. I only pray it will be strong enough."

Nodding, "It will be very strong."

Picking Timmy up Stoney carries him out of the house with Evening Star and Cindy following, when Evening Star asks. "Shall I get the car?"

"We should walk as our ancestors walked."

As they approach the sacred circle they encounter hundreds of Navajo who respectively part, allowing them to pass.

Stoney enters the medicine Hogan carrying Timmy, completely ignoring the two *Hataalii* holy men and their assistants, who are assembling the huge sand painting on the floor. The top of the painting is facing east, toward the Hogan's entryway, as a preventive measure, to prevent evil spirits who may enter through the doorway from entering the sand painting.

After placing Tim, wrapped in the white blanket, near the fire then lighting some sage in a brightly colored bowl, he moves around Tim, cleansing and purifying him with the sacred smoke then repeating the ceremony with Cindy and Evening Star.

The cleansing ceremony complete, he sits across the fire from Tim, and motions for Cindy to sit on his left and Evening Star on his right. The fire is casting it's reflection on the massive timbers of the Hogan.

Looking at Cindy, we see both concern and confusion... Her attention is drawn to the fire when Stoney raises his hands above the fire and begins to chant and, startled, when the flames suddenly increase in height and density.

First confused, then utterly amazed, she watches the image of an old Indian appear in the flames, Black Eagle. Cindy is almost spellbound as she watches Black Eagle chant, while holding his hands over a fire and dropping three small eagle feathers into the flames. She watches as they suddenly burst into flame, only to reappear as they gently float above the fire, slowly rising. Floating up and out through the smoke hole of his lodge, then almost instantly reappearing in their Hogan, gently floating above Tim, where they slowly settle on his white blanket and dissolve into ash from Black Eagle's sacred fire..

While John, sitting at his desk and trying to concentrate on papers scattered over his desk, is finding it almost impossible to concentrate on anything except the talking drums.

Finally shaking his head and pushing his papers aside, "I give up, I can't think about anything except those drums"

"I've checked all the windows and they are all closed. Would it help if I made some hot chocolate for you?"

"No thank you, I think the only thing that will help is for us to go over there and find out what's going on."

"Do you really feel that's necessary?"

Nodding, "Yes, I can't explain it, but I feel like those drums are calling us. Just give me a few minutes while I change my clothes."

John hurriedly begins changing his clothes, putting on a well-worn pair of jeans a western hat and an old pair of boots and an old western shirt. Looking in the mirror he kind of likes what he sees, except "I don't think I'll need these." John begins removing his rings, gold chains and Rolex watch.

Seeing what he's doing, Peggy opens her dresser drawer and removes an old wooden box, which she first holds close to her breast, as if giving thanks to the Great Spirit, then setting the box on her dresser opens it and reverently removes something. Without saying a word, hands it to John... who is stunned when he sees what she's just handed him... "Where in the world did you ever get this? It's my old medicine bag. I haven't seen it in over twenty years."

Nodding, "I know, your mother gave it to me years ago, before she passed away. She asked me to keep it for you, because she knew that someday you would want to wear it again."

Peggy takes it from his hand and places it around his neck.

Looking in the mirror, John says, "Yes, she was right and I should never have taken it off, for it feels like it belongs there."

Then, turning to look at his wife, he pauses while absorbing her beauty. Her beautiful raven black hair hanging down her back almost to her waist, the sparkle of her eyes and dressed so simply, in a long dress almost to her ankles with a small band tied around her neck and a long white shawl, folded and draped over her delicate arm, her beauty, as always, astounds him. Smiling at her, he picks up his hat and takes her arm.

"Shall we go visiting?"

They drive one of the ranch jeeps down the little dirt road, and are surprised to find dozens upon dozens of parked cars, pickup trucks, and even two eighteen wheeler truck and trailers parked at the end of the road. In amazement, John asks, "What in the world is going on?"

Standing on the edge of the cliff where they can look down into Black Eagle's camp, they are both shocked and amazed. The scene unfolding before their eyes is like looking into the annals of history… Their history, their ancient history, hundreds, if not thousands of years in their ancestors past, a history that makes their hearts swell with pride. As they find themselves looking into a heritage they have not given much thought to since they were children.

Suddenly they realize it is a heritage they are proud of… A heritage they will never allow themselves to forget, ever again.

Dozens upon dozens, of Native American Indians from almost every tribe imaginable. Shoshone, Iroquois, Cherokee, Comanche, Arapahoe, Kiowa, Blackfoot, Apache, Sioux, Kickapoo, Zuni, Choctaw, Crow, and Fox many in their traditional regalia, are singing and dancing in the sacred arena to the beat of a mother drum and eight drummers, two sets of four, a sacred number, around a blazing ceremonial fire.

"Oh John, it's so beautiful… Lets hurry, I want to see my father."

"Where do you think he is?"

"I don't see him by the sacred circle, so he's probably in his tepee."

Peggy and john hurry down the trail and across the stream and up the little hill to Black Eagle's tepee and stepping in, they find Black Eagle sitting by his fire, smoking his sacred pipe.

Without looking up, "I've been expecting you."

John and Peggy both slip moccasins on, and take a seat by the fire as indicated by Black Eagle

When they're seated, Peggy asks, "Caroline told us you were having a medicine dance. Who is the dance for?"

"For a little child and all of us."

"What's wrong with the child?"

"Leukemia."

"Oh, No." Then, "Where is this child?"

"On the Navajo reservation in New Mexico."

John asks. "You said the medicine dance was for all of us. What do you mean all of us?"

Motioning toward the fire, Black Eagle answers, "Look into the fire for your answer."

As Black Eagle raises his hands above the fire, the flames suddenly leap into the air, and both Peggy and John's gaze is immediately drawn to the image that appears in the flames…Stoney in his white ceremonial regalia of White Buffalo.

John stiffens… Peggy reaches over and gives his hand a squeeze.

Peggy is the first to speak. "That's… Stoney.

"No, it is White Buffalo."

Peggy and John look at each other with bewilderment, then back to the image in the fire. Finding it extremely difficult, to believe what they are seeing is their son performing a healing ceremony on the Navajo reservation in New Mexico. The drummers suddenly increase the tempo of their drumming.

Slowly shaking his head, John asks," I don't understand, what do you mean, White Buffalo?"

"Do you not remember the tales of White Buffalo you heard as a child?"

"Of course I do, every Indian child has heard the stories about White Buffalo. But that's all they were, stories nothing more."

"Not quite, they were stories yes, but they were stories from our past, from our heritage… They are true stories of our great heritage."

After puffing on his sacred pipe,"This medicine dance tonight is not only Navajo and Cherokee; it is a healing dance for us all. This dance is a gathering of the Nations, and is being danced and sung by every tribe in every sacred circle throughout the land, The Apache, Sioux, Dineh, Seminole, Cheyenne, Ojibwa, Chumash, Apache, Creeks, Kickapoo, Chickasaws, Crow, Mohawk, Cree, Paiute, Shoshone, Ute, Arapaho, Potawatomi, Comanche, Seneca, and Tuscarora have all gathered to dance this dance tonight.

For it is not only to help cure this little boy with leukemia, it is a curing process for all of us, to show the Great Spirit we are worthy of the Return of White Buffalo."

"The Return of White Buffalo…" John asks in amazement, "But.. But why Stoney?"

"He was chosen by the Great Spirit even before he was born, and has proven himself to be a worthy warrior in everything he has done. He cares about all creatures and has always put the welfare of others before his own. Have you ever known him to ever say anything except the truth?" Not waiting for an answer, "No, because he feels to lie is a sign of weakness.

You should be proud of your son, and you of all people should know why he was chosen, you raised him."

There are tears of pride in Peggy's eyes as John asks.

"What can we do to help?"

"Believe in him, believe as he believes."

Peggy looks back into the fire with tears glistening in her eyes, Black Eagle smiles.

"Have you forgotten your heritage so soon? Indian women do not shed tears in public."

Looking at her father with determination, "These are tears of pride, and I'm proud of them."

Peggy gasps as John asks, "Will Stoney ever come back to us?"

"Of course, this is his home, and he will return whenever he can." and pausing with a smile, "I believe he did mention something about a camping trip."

"Then I better get busy and buy a new sleeping bag."

"No, you better buy two of them, because I'm going with you." Peggy tells him.

Smiling to herself, Peggy returns her attention to the fire to watch her son as he...

Battle Shield

Native Americans believe dancing is prayer, opening a doorway to our creator, an offering to our creator.

22

Mountain Chant Healing Ceremony

...Picks Tim up, and with Cindy and Evening star
following, carry him out to the sacred circle.

A large fire is burning in the center of the sacred circle,
sending its burning embers into the night sky. A dozen or so
dancers, each carrying arrows in their hands, are dancing a
very intricate step to the beat of the drum.

While Stoney is preparing for the Hunters dance, Willie Pale
Deer has been listening to the drums and getting more and
more desperate. Shouting to the two figures hiding in the
shadows, "How could they do this? How could they do this?
They are going to ruin everything, everything I've worked so
hard for." Turning to look at his two Skinwalkers, "I won't let
them get away with it." Opening a cupboard, Pale Deer
rummages through the clutter of little packages and vials. A
smile crosses his face as he finds the vial he is searching for
and turning to his skinwalkers, "Hurry. Get the black candles,
and bring them to me. Hurry, hurry before it's too late." The
skinwalkers bring Pale Deer five large black candles, which he
lights and places on the flimsy little kitchen table around the
sand painting of Jim Light Horse Morris and his son Tim.
"Now let's see if they dare interfere with this." Sitting back,
the witch says, "I'll show him." Gazing at the sand painting,

the witch begins chanting an almost forgotten, ancient ritual, while sprinkling herbs into the flames of the black candles. The two skinwalkers quietly slip back into the shadows.

Stoney pauses and, turning first toward the drummers and singers then the dancers, raises Tim in his outstretched hands, honoring the drummers and dancers, then steps into the sacred circle, holding Tim's seemingly lifeless form straight out in his arms. Suddenly, Stoney feels as if his body were turning to lead, Timmy's little form suddenly becomes a great weight, trying to force him to lower his arms, to force him to lower Timmy. The muscles in his arms begin to burn. Gritting his teeth, Stoney refuses to give in to this new threat from the Witch. Raising his head, he quietly asks the Great Spirit to give him the strength of the White Buffalo, and almost effortlessly, Stoney raises Tim even higher.

The dancers move closer, they begin dancing around Stoney and the child. The dancers wave their arrows above their heads while chanting their prayers. They wave their arrows above and below the child, they gently touch him with their arrows. They touch him on his elbow, his foot, his stomach, his head and his back. Over and over again, they touch every part of his body.

Evening star is quietly explaining to Cindy what they are doing as Black Eagle is explaining to John and Peggy.

"This is the Hunter's Dance; the dancers are touching every part of the child's body with their arrows, to drive the evil spirits and illness from every part of his body."

John asks, "Evil spirits?"

"Yes, bad medicine, evil spirits. A Navajo Witch and his Skinwalkers have cast a spell on this child."

The dancers soon move away from Stoney and the child. Stoney carries the child back into the Hogan and places him in the center of the now finished sand painting, which depicts the history of Raised Within The Mountains, and on each side of the painting, images representing the four sacred mountains of the Navajo.

Two healers step forward and immediately begin chanting prayers while placing small sacrifices of sacred corn pollen and flower pedals on Tim's unmoving form, while the drumming, dancing and singing continues, both in and around the sacred circle.

The hundreds and hundreds of Navajo gathered around the sacred circle begin to sing and dance. Men women and children alike offer their voices in prayer to the Great Spirit for this child's healing.

While at the trailer, Pale Deer is in a rage, pulling his hair and shouting, "He can't do that, he can't do that, no one can do that." Then turning to his Skinwalkers, he demands, "Go down there, go down there and find out how they are doing this to me and if you can find a way to get rid of that little whelp once and for all. Do it and do it quick." As the skinwalkers, hurriedly open the door to leave. A powerful gust of wind, seemingly out of nowhere, enters the trailer, and as easily as a giant would blow grains of sand from the palm of his hand, the sand painting is, blown away.

"Shut the door, shut the door." Pale Deer screams as he frantically tries to save something from his sand painting. Seeing the fury in Pale Deer's eyes, and well aware of their masters temper, the Skinwalkers assume the form of dogs and with their tails between their legs, flee to the dark safety of the cedar trees. Frustrated and angry, Pale Deer jumps up from the table and runs after them, screaming, "Come back, come back." Not realizing that in his haste, he bumped the flimsy table, knocking two of the black candles over, one falling to the trash littered floor, the other rolling over to the old cotton curtains. Spreading quickly through the trash and debris, the trailer is soon, engulfed in flames. Pale Deer, unaware of the fire, searches frantically through the trees for his Skinwalkers, until, finally noticing the bright glow of flames on the trees. Pale Deer turns in disbelief, as he sees his potions, herbs and formulas, his entire life going up in flames.

Dropping to his knees, Pale Deer begins pounding mother earth with his fists as he screams, "It's gone! It's gone, everything is gone!

Chanting prayers for this child's healing, Stoney gazes into the fire, its flames reflected in the thin layer of perspiration coating his forehead.

The ceremony continues hour after hour, suddenly the drumming and chants become louder. Tim stirs while lying on the sacred sand painting Cindy starts to get up, and Stoney puts a slight restraining hand on her shoulder. Standing himself, he walks over to the child, picking him up, and once again carries him out to the sacred circle for the Fire Dance… Seeing Stoney approach with the child, the drummers and dancers intensify their efforts.

Yet the only sounds are from the drums and the crackling of the sacred fire. Everyone else seems to be holding their breath. Carrying the child, Stoney steps into the center of the sacred circle and stands next to the sacred fire. He slowly raises the child aloft, as if offering this child to the Supreme Being.

The healers begin their Mountain chant, a formula that has been passed down from healer to healer for thousands of years, every word and every nuance in its precise place.

As the chanting begins, to a soft almost non-existent beat of the drum, Fire dancers appear, slowly approaching single file out of the darkness beyond the sacred circle. The drummers softly begin singing their prayers as they slowly increase the beat of the drum, as the fire dancers approach the sacred circle. Steadily increasing their drumming as the fire dancers begin circling the sacred circle, dancing closer and closer to the east side of the circle where they will enter. Their bodies begin to pick up the reflection of the fire.

Soon the sacred, flames can be seen glistening on their painted bodies, which are covered only with paint of their sacred colors, slowly dancing closer and closer to the sacred circle. Each dancer is carrying a wand covered with eagle down, which he raises and lowers as he gently strikes the back of the dancer in front, and then gently striking his own back.

Everyone seems mesmerized, as they watch this most sacred of sacred dances.

Each step in its exact place to the exact beat of the drum, each wave of their wands exactly as it was prescribed, thousands of years ago, always moving forward, never turning around or looking back.

The dancers reach the sacred circle and enter to a crescendo of the drum, moving slowly to the left, clockwise around the sacred fire. The healers continuing their chant as the fire dancers make a wide circle around Stoney and the child, completely ignoring their presence.

The dancers continue circling, making each circle a little smaller, drawing their dance circle closer and closer to Stoney, the child and the sacred fire, while continuing to gently strike the dancer in front on his back with their holy wands, then striking their own backs. The dancers wave their sacred wands toward the child, as Stoney remains motionless, holding the child in a raised position toward the night sky, toward the Great Spirit.

When their circle becomes small enough for them to reach the sacred fire, they light their sacred wands in the sacred fire and continue striking the dancer in front then, striking their own backs and waving their flaming wands toward the child.

When a wand is extinguished from either waving or striking, the wand is immediately re-lighted in the sacred fire. No dancer ever turns or looks back, they always look forward.

When a dancer's wand is no longer long enough to be held in the dancer's hand, the remnants of the wand are thrown into the sacred fire, to be consumed in its sacred flames as the dancer runs screaming from the sacred circle.

As this occurs, the Navajos supporting this sacred dance with their prayers scream taunts at the dancer, as if chasing him from the sacred circle.

They begin dancing themselves and soon every Navajo there, men, women and children alike, are dancing this prayer for this child.

As their wands burn up and the dancers flee, fewer and fewer dancers remain, until finally only Stoney remains in the sacred circle, still holding the child raised in his hands.

Chief Dragging Canoe would ask. Where have our warriors gone?

23

Return of White Buffalo

As the last fire dancer flees the sacred circle, the Navajos begin to notice a bright glow appearing around the figure holding the child.

The glow appears to be getting brighter and brighter, as a vision begins forming. A vision that is appearing throughout the country in every sacred circle of every tribe throughout the land, telling all tribes the Great Spirit has returned White Buffalo's powers.

First appearing as a small, glowing ball, almost as if it were a firefly, appearing to float gently in the air, as it slowly circles the figure standing in the sacred circle. The little ball gradually grows larger and larger, brighter and brighter.

Until suddenly, with an almost blinding flash, a White Buffalo appears, standing at Stoney's side it's huge size dwarfing Stoney as he stands un-moving holding the child extended toward the Great Spirit.

The White Buffalo's eyes are glowing like red-hot coals, as it paws mother earth, with vapor exploding from his nostrils, tossing his huge horned head. Slowly, the earth beneath their feet begins to tremble and rumble, gradually increasing. The leaves in the trees begin to shake as the trembling of mother earth increases, a dust cloud appears to be rising from over the hillside above the sacred circle.

Suddenly, the thunderous rumble of forty thousand hoofs are reverberating through mother earth, as ten thousand buffalo appear, blackening the hillside. A sight that has not been seen for almost two hundred years

Spellbound the Navajo gasp in amazement, as the night sky suddenly erupts with the flash of lightning, so bright it turns night into day, and the crack of thunder so loud it seems to make even the mighty trees tremble as it rolls across the countryside.

Then suddenly it is gone, and all is quiet. Only the one glowing figure remains in the sacred circle, still holding the child extended toward the night sky, toward the Great Spirit.

Slowly lowering the child, Stoney turns and walks slowly to a stunned Cindy and Evening Star, handing Tim to his mother.

"The Great Spirit has given you back your son." As Tim stirs in her arms. "All he needs now is rest."

There are tears in Cindy's eyes and gratitude in the eyes of Evening Star as the drummers and dancers begin a new dance, a dance of celebration...

A dance of celebration like no other celebration held in thousands of years past. Even the children join in, celebrating the Return of White Buffalo.

And at Black Eagle Valley. Peggy stands and proudly announces, "I wish to join the dancers, for I wish to celebrate White Buffalo's return of with our people."

Black Eagle nods, "I think we should all dance, for it is said when the Cherokee no longer dance the sun will no longer rise and the seasons will no longer change."

Several days later, Stoney's pickup truck and horse trailer are parked in front of Evening Star's house.
Cindy and Evening Star are helping Stoney load some gear into his truck, while Timmy is picking handfuls of grass to feed Roamer.

Evening Star is giving Stoney a very beautiful white blanket.

"I saw a very beautiful woman in your healing fire and, if I'm not mistaken, she had just the twinkle of a tear in her eyes, which leads me to believe she is you're mother. I would like you to give this blanket to her with my gratitude for sharing her wonderful son with us."

"Thank you Evening Star, I'll see that she receives your most gracious gift." Then, turning to Cindy, asks, "Are you going to be all right?"

Putting her arms around Evening Star while smiling, "You don't have to worry about me or Tim anymore, I've got more than I could have ever hoped for. A home with a brand new wonderful mother, the Evening Star I've been wishing on all my life, a healthy son who is going to be starting school very soon right here on the reservation, and the biggest family in the world, the whole Navajo Nation. And Sally was by yesterday to tell me Lou can't wait to have me back, and with a raise yet. So yes, Stoney, thanks to you, I am finally going to be all right. And now, that you don't have me and Tim to worry about any more, what are you going to be doing?"

With a smile, "I thought I just might do a little camping."

Donadagohvi.   Until we meet again.

About the Author

Known as the Dream Catcher, Charles Fivekiller believes no race of people have endured more or have more to be proud of than Native Americans. Lives, in what he refers to as Paiute and Shoshone country on the high, desert of Southern California. Surrounded by four sacred Buttes, with his son Thomas, their horses and three dogs and where, if you happen to be in the neighborhood, and hear the drums. You are more than welcome to join them and their many Native American friends for one of their drumming and sings

A General Contractor and General Engineering Contractor licensed in two States, turned author, is the author of several novels, none of which is closer to his heart than the "Return of White Buffalo," which he hopes will bring better understanding of our wonderful American Indian heritage and culture to people of all color.

As he believes it was through ignorance brought on by our lack of understanding each others culture that allowed some of the most horrendous tragedies in the annals of American history to occur, to mention only a few.

The Trail of Tears, Wounded Knee, the Long Walk, Sand Creek, Washita, the massacre of Tohopeka and the almost unmentioned Marias Massacre...

He also believes we must never allow ourselves to forget these dark days in our history. For it is through tragedies such as these that native people have gained the courage and strength, to overcome the many adversities they have had to face. He believes it is time we used our courage and strength to rekindle the warrior spirit in all our young modern day warriors, so they may build a brighter future for all native people.

Let us pray, the Great Spirit will grant us all, red, white, brown, yellow and black, the wisdom to recognize our mistakes and allow us the ability to understand each other's ways, and grant us the strength to never allow such senseless tragedies to occur, ever again, to any race of people.

The Author

To contact the author E-mail charlesbreulauthor@yahoo.com

To visit White Buffalo's web site
www.returnofwhitebuffalo.com

For those who may feel parts of this book may be politically incorrect or politically motivated or in condemnation of others, I apologize, for this was never my intention. It is only my desire to bring to light a few of the many tragedies Native Americans have endured, throughout history in silence.

To be able to tell our side of these tragedies as they actually occurred, as described, not by a biased media, but by people who were actually there, by the survivors of these tragedies, the survivors of these holocausts.

Charles Fivekiller Breul

Camelot Publishing
The Cutting edge

Quick Order Form

A Gift for a Friend

Please accept White Buffalo's invitation
To Visit his Web Site
www.returnofwhitebuffalo.com

A GIFT FOR A FRIEND
Quick Order Form

Fax orders: 661 264- 4180 Please send this form
Telephone orders: Call 866 356 - 9574 Toll free
For discounts on multiple books, call 866 356 - 9574 Toll free
E-mail orders: camelotpublishing@hotmail.com
Snail mail: P.O. Box 500057 Lake Los Angeles, Ca. 93535
          Please send this form
Please send the following books and or disks.
Single copies may also be ordered from popular online
bookstores as well as many online tribal bookstores, which we
urge you to support.
<u>**Return of White Buffalo, Book I**</u> $14.95__ , **Disk** $14.95___
Please send free information on: Please check selections
Other books_____ Author tours and book signings_____
Name:_____
Address: _____
City: _____ **State:**_____ **Zip:**_____
Telephone:_____
E-mail address:_____
Sales tax: Please add 8.25% for products sent to California
Shipping and handling by air: U.S.: $4.00 for first book or
disk and $2.00 for each additional product. $_____
International: $9.00 for first book or disk: $5.00 for each
additional product $_____
Total amount $ _____
Payment: Check___, **Credit card; Visa**____ , **Amex**___,
Master card_____, **Optima** _____, **Discovery** _____
Card number_____
Code_____   **(Last three digits on back of card)**
Name on card: _____
Signature of cardholder _____
Exp. Date: _____
Wado (Thank you)